Roads without Houses

Roads without Houses

stories

Joseph Rein

Press 53
Winston-Salem

Press 53, LLC
PO Box 30314
Winston-Salem, NC 27130

First Edition

Cover design by Kevin Morgan Watson

Cover image Copyright © 2017
by William Rein, used by permission of the artist.

Author photo by William Rein

Library of Congresss Control Number 2017958985

Printed on acid-free paper
ISBN 978-1-941209-71-4

For Jessica, who makes all things possible

The author thanks the editors of the publications where the following stories first appeared:

Concho River Review, "Kindred's Mother"

Fiction Weekly, "To Play Hockey, One-on-One"

Hawai'i Review, "Intimations of Chloe"

Iron Horse Literary Review, "Danielle's Barn"

The Laurel Review, "Encyclopedia Alanica"

Prime Number Magazine, "Encyclopedia Helenica"

Wisconsin Review, "Building Faith"

Contents

Danielle's Barn

The woman asks for barnyard animals. It's not the oddest request Jason has received, but the woman still asks like a conspirator, pausing, laughing awkwardly, whispering even over the phone. She sounds young: mid-twenties, a bit older. Jason imagines her pacing and biting at painted fingernails.

"I can do that," Jason says. "No problem."

The woman doesn't respond. From the background comes a dim banging noise, the sound of hard plastics colliding over and over. "Asher, no," she says out of the phone. "Here, here." Then she's back, her breathing quickened. She nearly pants. "Okay, but just so I get this— so we're on the same page."

"Sure," Jason says. He listens for Asher, for little squeals or grunts. He thinks he hears a hiccup.

"You're okay with, like, dirt and stuff. On their faces. I want it to be really real."

"Whatever you want."

The woman discharges an exaggerated sigh through the phone. Behind her, a raucous little voice shouts the alphabet.

"Great," she says. "That's just great. When are you available?"

Jason picks up his appointment book, an old notebook with pink jewels halved and pasted around the edges. Three of the jewels have fallen off, leaving oblong smears of glue like uncooked egg white. Jason schedules her for next Tuesday, 2:00. Her name is Brianna. Through the phone, Asher starts to cry. Brianna ignores him.

"Great. Just one more question. Do I need to, like, bring anything?"

"Just your subjects," Jason says. It is supposed to be a joke but Brianna doesn't laugh. "The kids should be all. I usually get the outfits and any necessary props, back-drops. This one will be easy—"

Jason stops himself on that word: easy. He envisions varied moments from years ago, skies both sunny and overcast, his grass trimmed and untended. The barn both a pile of repurposed wood along the backyard shore of their lake home, stacked like a winterized dock, and then finally his carefully constructed play masterpiece. Danielle barely able to stand, Danielle running.

"I usually make backdrops," he says. "But I already have something. Something great for this."

"Fantastic. See you Tuesday."

She hangs up abruptly, cutting off her voice, her breathing, and Asher's cries all in one.

Charlotte never went into his darkroom. *It's spooky*, she told him shortly after he'd built it. *That red. Like Dracula's lair or something.* That's why Jason felt comfortable doing what he did: he never imagined Charlotte would find out.

From the start, Jason had pursued photography for the same reasons as everyone else: the artistry, the self-expression, the ability not only to see the world but to capture it, to seize moments at their most unembellished, their most vulnerable. Their most articulate. Then, like everyone else, he realized that artistry didn't make his car or rent or student loan payments. It didn't even buy the equipment necessary for its own creation. And then life hurled itself upon him, starting with the wedding, which Charlotte wanted to keep small but had still managed to sap most of their savings. Then the house, a modest one-story but with the enviable lakefront backyard, a mutual dream of Jason and Charlotte for which they sank too deep in debt. In little time, Jason found himself photographing low-rate models in jeans and t-shirts for department stores, or taking headshots of former Crivitz sports heroes for real-estate billboards. Lawn equipment and back-to-school supplies so brilliant he had to squint. He layered bedspreads, rearranged dining sets to accentuate their handcrafted edging. Soon enough he was capturing life only to sell it.

So he saved artistry for his personal photography. In a tiny section of their basement he built his windowless darkroom, which could only be accessed through a Lazy Susan-like entryway. Step in, half-turn of the opening, step out. In the comfort of red safelights, his developed pictures hung paper clipped to a wire like clothes drying in a setting sun. There was something romantic in these photos, something film captured that digital never could. Of course, he did all his commercial work on digital. He routinely snapped five hundred images at a shoot only to use one or two. Fiscally, practically, it made sense. But he hated the throwaway feel, the way you could see, critique, and discard an image in seconds. So many new photographers didn't even imagine before they shot. The digital pictures themselves also felt disingenuous: the grainy texture, the dark backlighting. Everything looked underwater, awash in blue. The pictures also lacked depth, like a movie shot entirely in front of a green screen. The technical term was pixilated, and other photographers would tell Jason he just wasn't doing it right. But he knew: his personal photos had simultaneously that old-world feel but also something more real.

That night, Jason had arrived home late from a shoot. Charlotte's car was in the garage, but she wasn't in the kitchen or living room or bedroom. He walked to the basement and heard a clang inside his darkroom. He entered the revolving door covered with glow-in-the-dark star stickers lumped into slapdash constellations. *To the moon!* he had shouted the first time, startling Danielle a bit, but soon enough she was squealing for more. *Moon daddy moon daddy moon daddy!* He rotated the opening and walked in.

The safelights shone stark red. The sliding tables had been moved. A spilled vial of acetic acid filled the air with a pungent chrome scent. Across the center of the room, his pictures hung on the wire like the teeth of an exaggerated smile. Except now there were two gaps, two pulled baby teeth, on either side. Through one of the gaps Jason saw Charlotte leaning on the back table, pictures in hand.

"Jason," she said. Her voice was sad, soft, conciliatory even. She breathed in deeply. Then her voice sharpened. "Why are you doing this to me?"

In her left hand she held an early photo of Danielle in her bouncer, her open mouth chasing a roving fist. In her right, not two years later, Danielle at the petting zoo, a soft wind pushing short blond bangs from her face, that same fist clasped around a quarter's worth of feed. Her blue eyes gazed just past the camera lens, maybe at the swarming goats, maybe her mother. Maybe him.

"Doctor Mancuso said we needed to slowly move things out. Not add more."

Jason stepped toward her. She hadn't looked up from the pictures. "Mancuso is a hack. He actually used the word purge, Char. Purge. As though she's some type of—poison. Like we need to cleanse ourselves."

Charlotte set the pictures down, taking care not to stack them, to touch only the edges. Then she walked past him and out of the room. He heard the stairs creak, the door open, her car start. He heard her leave and knew she wouldn't come home that night. He didn't know where she was going: her mother's, a motel. A lover's house possibly. Jason imagined Charlotte underneath this new, rapacious man, looking into his eyes and seeing something other than mutual pain.

He replaced the photos in their chronological order on the line. To the far left, the first week: at home in the living room, lying on a pink, monkey-patterned blanket, her crossed eyes fighting to focus. In the middle, fifteen months: a summer shot at the park, grabbing at a seesaw handle with innocent abandon. Finally, to the far right, just shy of three years: her playing in the barn. In her barn. Behind her, through slivers of pine needles, the lake shone with an unmistakable effervescence. Her head and shoulders peeked from the barn's only window, where her face reflected midday light inversely, almost from the bottom up. It was Jason's favorite picture of Danielle, and his last.

Brianna arrives late with Asher and his older brother, the alphabet-shouting Declan. Brianna is a bit older than

Jason imagined, mid-thirties, short but thin, with hints of gray in her controlled black hair. The boys are both under four, dressed in matching green flannel and jeans. Declan bolts past Jason to his pile of equipment. He makes a tornado valley of Jason's tripods and rolls of backdrops. With Asher in arm, Brianna attempts to scold Declan from afar but Jason just laughs.

"Don't worry, Miss Smith. That's really what they're for. Half the stuff here is play fodder."

"Bri." She sets Asher down on all fours to shake Jason's hand. "Everyone calls me Bri. Hell, even Declan does."

"That's good," Jason says. He points to Asher. "I mean your youngest. He's got the pose down already."

"If you can catch him. Blink and he's gone."

Jason goes to his garage and returns with an army duffel of props: fur hats, costume paints in all colors, hay purchased from a nearby farm. A yard waste bag full of dirt. He walks it all to the backyard, past his broken air conditioner and a landscape island overrun with clover, to the barn sitting amid overgrown grass.

"Wow," Brianna says. She shakes her head. "And dirt! This—my friend said you were good."

Jason accepts the compliment with silence. The parents always admire his diligence with props, his ability to turn patches of grass into a soccer pitch, outer space, a bistro. As Declan squints down the wrong end of an old lens, Asher beelines for the barn with surprising speed.

"Faster than his brother," Brianna says. "No joke. Ash honey, stay away from the water okay! Is it very deep?"

"No," Jason says. "Knee deep for a good stretch. It actually rises before it falls."

Asher stops just before the barn. He looks to Brianna as though awaiting permission. Then he carefully places both hands on the burnt-red wood, gets one leg and then both under him, and something in Jason's chest seizes. He nearly drops his camera. He wonders why he ever thought this was a good idea.

"Come here, little guy," Jason says softly. Walking over to Asher, he takes him a few feet from the barn. He retrieves the costume paint and focuses on turning Asher's face into a lamb's, the soft white cover, the dark nose, the dirt spots. Asher sits wide-eyed, surprisingly okay with Jason touching his face. When Brianna finally corrals Declan, Jason gives him the black spots and speckled ears of a calf. The boys notice each other and laugh.

"This," Brianna says, walking Asher to the barn again. "This'll be great."

At some point Jason began taking only small-children gigs, though he couldn't recall exactly when. As a courtesy to Charlotte he'd rented a studio in town. Still, she spent more nights away from home, sometimes returning only at dinnertime the next day. Each time Jason set a plate for her, he envisioned it going cold across from him, becoming cling-wrapped leftovers that would mold in the back of the fridge. But each time she came back, eating little and saying less.

The first few shoots were of the standard, Sears-type stuff: boys in collared shirts, girls in uncomfortable dresses and hairclips, full families in ceremonious poses and half-smiles. He charged little and the clients were moderately pleased. But then came the first peculiar request: the Ibsens, a middle-aged couple who looked like siblings, wanted pictures of their three girls in bikini tops and mermaid bottoms. *Could you Photoshop in an ocean scene too, in the background?* Mr. Ibsen asked, but Jason decided instead to paint his backdrop wall a turquoise-blue and add chunks of faux coral. The Ibsens gasped audibly when they saw it. After a half hour of shots, Mr. Ibsen took Jason aside and asked if he could somehow suspend his daughters in air. *You know, like they're swimming. Like actual mermaids.* Instead, Jason placed a few uneven wood crates underneath the blue floor drape and set the girls atop them. Mrs. Ibsen cooed like a child. The two older girls enjoyed this fake-floating, but argued over which should be highest. The youngest had to be strapped down and cried the whole time. To his standard, Jason hadn't gotten one decent shot, but before even seeing proofs, the Ibsens wrote Jason a check for five hundred dollars more than his sitting fee. He received a thank you card a few days after mailing the disc. *Everyone LOVES the photos! Their Nana nearly keeled over!* They referred Jason to a dozen other parents. This and subsequent shoots—two boys as police chiefs patrolling the streets, a three-month-old girl as a daisy in a field—confirmed to Jason that this market alone could carry him. It was the cuteness of the photos, yes, but even more, Jason suspected it was the imagination behind them, the fancy. The potential. The childhood ability to see the world as a wonderland, as awesomely possible. Jason's quirky photos of their children were like some secret drug, the thing these parents couldn't get enough of.

After a few weeks he showed Charlotte some of the photos. She looked at each for a minute, maybe more. They shook in her hands.

"They're beautiful," she finally said. She set them on the table and walked straight to her car.

The next day, she removed Danielle's old clothes from storage bins and folded them on the kitchen table. She spread foam blocks and stuffed animals on the living room floor as though Danielle had been playing with them. She opened old jars of baby food and ate them with tiny, plastic-tipped spoons. She turned Nickelodeon on the television and then left the room.

"I'm not doing it to hurt you," Jason said that night. He was on his side, facing Charlotte. She lay on her back, her eyes on the ceiling fan. "I never once—never—"

In a flash he lost all the words he thought to say to his wife, as though something had torn open the camera of his mind and exposed its film to light.

"I don't know," he said finally, "why you feel the need to punish me."

She closed her eyes. "I don't know either."

Jason ducks under his camera, his legs kicking, his lips puckered and cheeks flared in the best monkey impression he can muster. He shakes his whole body and feels the heaviness of a headache forming in his temples. Asher smiles at him; Declan watches his own feet. But Jason keeps snapping anyway, at least twenty shots before Asher turns away and paws again at the base of the barn. He catches a few good ones. In the distance, the sun's reflection off the lake creates the illusion of a country sunrise.

Through the shoot Brianna is less interested than Jason thought she would be. She spends most of the time running a finger across her phone, looking up only here and there to tell the boys to smile. Jason envisions this scene all across town: at the grocery store, at parks. At fireworks over the lake on the Fourth of July. He wonders how many times she's lost one of them in a crowded place. But then he stops himself, realizing that he does this with every mother whose children he photographs: he compares them unfavorably, unfairly, to Charlotte.

Like this, a moment that proves he is being unfair: Asher grabs at his brother's foot and Declan kicks it crudely away. Asher falls to his back and cries. In an instant Brianna pockets the phone and is on them, soothing Asher with her hands, scolding Declan softly with her eyes. She hasn't said a word, and yet both boys feel exactly what they should. They cling to her with the calm fervor of loved children. It is these moments he misses most with Charlotte, the times of instinctive devotion, of inherent, motherly grace.

Once Danielle arrived, the lake's immediacy began to frighten Charlotte. *You can fence off a pool,* she would say, as though they had an option between the two. She recounted the local tale they'd both heard since they were young, of the girl who attempted to swim clear across the lake and drowned. That although it was rarely deeper than an adult, Lake Noquebay held the same preternatural, carnal appetites of bodies of water everywhere. The lake. It was always the lake.

But then came the calls. He was on some job having to do with home exercise equipment. Whether it was treadmills or weight benches, whether he had male or female models or none at all, he can't recall. But what he does remember: three missed calls in italicized blue on his phone, 3:13, 3:14, and 3:14 again, like bible passages. Irrelevant images, but there they are, the times in digital blue, flashing in his mind.

When he found a minute to call Charlotte back, a different female voice answered. "Mr. Black?" the voice said. It was a young voice, hesitant, a high school kid at best. Jason took too long to respond. "I'm—my name is Stacy. The lifeguard." Only then did Jason remember the picnic plans with Charlotte's friends, the pool afterwards.

"Where is Charlotte?" Jason asked. "Is my daughter okay?"

The girl gasped into the phone, and Jason knew.

At the hospital a string of nurses couldn't find the right doctor. When they finally did, a Doctor Samson, she approached in mismatched green scrubs. She seemed shorter than a doctor ought to be. She said all the things Jason didn't want to hear, *Half a minute at most* and *Take in water so fast at that age* and *Responders did all they could.* And finally: *Your wife is in 107. She's—she's not doing well.*

Jason stared down the hallway. Dr. Samson tried to lead him but he didn't move. She excused herself, and Jason just stood, his eyes on the flood of nurses and visitors and wheelchair patients and movement and life. At the end of that hall, in a room somewhere, his daughter—the little girl who had just that morning, for the first time, recited "Twinkle Twinkle Little Star" to him in full—lay lifeless. At the end of that hall, in another room, his wife cried alone.

At some point, the boys forget about him and just play. Declan has finally embraced his role as a calf, mooing and bumping the barn walls and chomping Brianna's dried fruits like cud. Jason gets some of his best pictures in these moments, his camera ceaselessly shuttering.

But then Declan peeks his head out the window. Jason's fingers lock onto the camera. As he looks up Declan smiles, his face illumined by the white trim. Jason's arms become impossibly heavy. He leans into a nearby tripod but its legs buckle and he falls forward. The camera lens cracks on the ground. The battery and memory card leap out onto the lawn.

"Oh!" Brianna says from somewhere. Jason lifts his head and brushes a prickly feeling from his neck. The boys have emerged from the barn, staring.

"Are you okay, Jason?" Brianna says.

"Yes." Jason gets to his knees, shakes his head. "I don't know—"

Brianna places her hand on his forearm. "Maybe you should sit down."

"No, really. I think—I think I'm okay."

"Do you need some water? We have a bottle in the car."

Before Jason can object, Brianna runs to the car. She rummages through piles of action figures and books and sippy cups on the floor. She emerges with a half-drank, lukewarm bottle of water. Jason accepts it.

"I'm sorry." She brings Asher into her arms. Declan hugs her leg. "And your camera! We can come back another time."

"No, no." He lifts the tripod back to its feet. "I don't want to inconvenience you." He replaces the memory card and reboots his camera. Through the spider-web crack on his lens his backyard looks shattered, surreal. He flips to the viewer, where Declan's face smiles through the barn window. He quickly moves to a different sequence.

"See," he says. "The lens is toast, but the card survived. We got some good stuff here." Jason taps the panel, as though this will convince Brianna. "I'll email you proofs tonight."

Brianna insists on paying upfront. Back at the car, she buckles in her boys—her calf and lamb, still painted and dirtier than before—and turns to Jason.

"Sorry again," she says.

"You didn't do anything."

"I know, but—" She puts a hand on his. Then she gets in her car and drives away.

That night, he sits at his computer while ice melts into his whiskey. An oscillating fan splashes him with intermittent bursts of air. His email is open, a blank message to brismith33@gmail.com on his screen. He plugs in the memory card, looks at the file names but doesn't open them. He usually never thinks about his pictures once he touches them up and sends them, never considers what becomes of them, but these he can see clearly: the two boys in his daughter's barn displayed on Brianna's work desk, speckled on the cover of graduation scrapbooks, blown up and framed over the house mantle. Projected to a captive audience at Asher's wedding. He sees them in the hand of an elderly Declan, a granddaughter atop his lap. They share a laugh as the little girl doubts her grandpa was ever so young.

Jason drinks the entire glass and closes his eyes, waiting for the liquor to go to his head. When it doesn't, he drags his cursor over every one of Brianna's pictures and deletes them.

She had left every light in the house on. That's how Jason knew. The foyer, the living room, both sides of the kitchen. The steps leading down to the basement, the hallway, their bedroom. Her walk-in closet shone with the unnatural white of fluorescent bulbs. He had envisioned her taking all of her clothes, but most of her blouses and jeans still hung on the metal rod. Four pairs of shoes sat scattered on the carpet.

He knelt under the exposing lights. He understood, in some abstract way, why she was gone. He knew her grieving process included some impenetrable need to be without him. That, to her, he hadn't suffered as much as she did. He had never blamed her for the accident, but he also understood how little that mattered. They were, to each other, a constant reminder of suffering, of remorse. Perhaps that's why so few parents stayed together after. Perhaps that's why, though her closet was still half full, he knew Charlotte wasn't coming back, knew it in the part of him that knew things instinctively, like the lens length for a perfect aerial shot, or the animal sound that could appease a fussy infant, or the fact that a little girl's— his little girl's, his Danielle's—impossibly incandescent moment could never be taken from him. The way Charlotte used to know him, how she had seen exactly him the moment after he'd taken the petting zoo photo and smiled at her.

"Don't say it."

Jason looked at his wife. She wore a yellow sundress, a hand-me-down from her deceased grandmother. She was beautiful.

"Don't say what?"

"Every kid loves animals. So every parent says it: *Gonna be a vet.*" She smiled back at him. "If kids chose their occupations at two, we'd have a world of healthy dachsunds and nothing else."

Jason didn't reply. Charlotte turned back to Danielle, who offered her closed fist to a pack of disinterested rabbits. Jason watched Charlotte, astonished that she knew, to the word, to the inflection in his voice, what he was going to say. He should have taken that picture—his wife watching his daughter, the sundress and the overfed rabbits and the crisp, crisp sky—but he had just stared, amazed, in awe of all the world had given him.

Running Home

When Steve took off running, it seemed he might never stop. It was hot for March: the syrupy air left a film on Reyna's forehead, on her fingertips. She watched Bill's shoe peel tar off the road, imagining a child's gum, pink and bubbly. He tromped with an air of undeserved grandeur. The three closed in on the tent, large and red-striped in the way carnival tents always were, though to Reyna it felt as though it were closing in on them.

"Gonna be late," Steve called over his shoulder. He ran with arms swinging stupidly at his sides. His feet landed in no particular place, his body spinning like a sideways Ferris Wheel. He had always moved this way, as though he'd been taught from a young age to occupy as much space as he could in the world.

"There is no late," Bill said, his steps bold, his voice breaking on *late*. He coughed and tapped at his throat, trying to cover up the fact that he was still, at sixteen, maturing. "They're not going anywhere till morning. That's how carnivals work."

Steve had somehow circled back to them. "Like you know how carnivals work."

"Rey's quiet," Bill said, turning their attention to her. His light brown hair had a childish curl that would stay, even as he grew old. When they were adults. Would they still be with the carnival then? Reyna had a hard time imagining it.

"Misses her mommy, I bet," Steve said.

"Shut up," Reyna said, quickening her step. Steve knew her mother: divorced, unemployed, grossly overweight, alcoholic. A string of malingering boyfriends. Reyna punched Steve on the shoulder, wanting to show she was just as serious as they were. The impact shuddered down her arm.

Because Steve couldn't hit Reyna back he hit Bill instead, prompting one of their boyish push-and-pull fights where they did little more than laugh and circle each other like prizefighters. Steve's hand tugging Bill's shoulder, Bill's elbow jabbing Steve's stomach: it was almost choreographed. When they looked up at the tent again, they stopped their dance and continued forward, as though just now remembering that they were abandoning their northwoods Wisconsin town and their lives for the road, perhaps forever.

"Now or never," Bill said to Reyna without looking back.

"The world at your fingertips," Steve added.

Blown-up words. Words for some imagined audience. The two had that way about them, obvious to anyone who'd spent half the time Reyna had spent with them: they lived like characters spouting clever lines written for moments like this. Relentlessly trying to out-charm each other. It was like watching a constant Brando picture. Bill the doting boyfriend, the caregiver. The trusting one. Steve the best friend, the confidant. The always-there-when-you-needed-him. In the back of his mind, Steve probably even envisioned some late-night lover's tryst between him and Reyna to set the complicated triangle in motion. *But we can't*, he would say between aggressive kisses. *Bill's my best friend.*

At the tent they stopped, surprised at the absence of someone to greet them. In the air hung a distant noise, like somewhere very close things were really happening. Reyna wondered what they should do now. Then she wondered how many times, in the near or distant future, that exact question would come to her.

Before she could ask, a lanky mustachioed man strutted past. He observed the three without interest, as though around every corner stood three people he didn't know and shouldn't care about. He would have continued right on walking if Steve hadn't waved.

"Hello? Excuse us?"

The man stopped. Meticulously groomed, his dyed moustache glimmered dead-of-night black.

"We're here to join." This was Bill. He put a hand on Steve's back and stepped ahead, as though to say *I'll take it from here.*

The man approached the two boys, hobbling on stilt-like legs. He didn't seem to have knees. Reyna had never met her father, but imagined him to be a man much like this one.

"We want to join," Bill repeated. "You know. The carnival."

Reyna waited for the man to laugh, or harrumph, or shoo them away. But he just stared, looking each of them up and down. Reyna would have felt exposed, conscious of her forming breasts and bared legs, but there was no sex in his stare. He sized them up like cattle at an auction.

"In the back," he said finally. "Talk to Skinny Jim."

As they passed him he added in a deadpan voice, as though he'd said it to a hundred kids before them, "Welcome to the Bombay Brothers' Boomtasmic Carnival."

Long-haired, tall as well, and younger than Reyna had expected, Skinny Jim smiled as Bill explained their intentions. Two of his teeth were crowned in gold. Saying nothing, he pushed a ballpoint pen and a thin piece of paper across the picnic table. Bill was the first—always the first—to sign over a scant dotted line. Reyna went last. *Colette Clowning*, she wrote with her off hand. Skinny Jim looked at it once. If he was at all suspicious of the name he didn't show it. Either that or he didn't care.

Gifted List Booksellers is one of a dying breed: thick carpets, low ceilings, dim lighting. Tenant of a boutique strip mall alongside stores that sell designer baby clothes and vintage furniture. When Milwaukee faithful describe it to Reyna they use the words *quaint* and *charming*. The big chains would have run Gifted List out of business long ago were it not for the authors it welcomes weekly, its sampling ranging from the obscure to the moderately infamous. Reyna had passed the store for years on her daily route without any interest in hearing an author read—the turtlenecks and blazers, the mock humility—until its owners reached down into her past, into, seemingly, her heart, to pull out the one treasure she'd buried there all those years ago. The treasure she'd run away from, the one she'd hoped for and then given up on, day after day. The treasure that taught her how exhausting, how impossibly endless, hope could be.

But here her treasure appears, and all the lost hope

with it, on the blue-and-red-dusted chalkboard outside the brick building, just above an advertisement for 30% off role-play dice games:

Here Tonight!!!
Author of Colette Clowning and Her
Mischievous Men! A Carnival Tale
7:30 Reading, 8:30 Signing

And then, in even bolder lettering, his name.

From that first day everyone called her C.C., Bill and Steve and the rest of the carnival crew. The only one who didn't was Skinny Jim, because they never saw him again. He proved a constant yet invisible presence, always behind a closed trailer door or a curtain, like the Wizard of Oz.

C.C. It wore on Reyna like an ill-fitting shirt. The result of a new identity and home overnight had a sobering effect on her. She caught herself whispering her real name when no one else was around, just to hear it aloud. *Reyna. Reyna.*

But to everyone else it was C.C., even the lanky mustachioed man who on most days commanded the pony rides. He wore tawdry harlequin pants and stuffed his crotch with the same yellowed tube sock. Without Skinny Jim he was also, for all intents and purposes, their boss. Every day he walked them through an unimpressive yet mobile lot—pickup trucks with hitches and faded-paint wooden booths on wheels—to explicate their next task.

"Bill, Steve, drag them hitches down the hill," he said, his mustache between his fingers like a cigarette. "C.C., pony detail."

This meant two things: feeding the five brown-and-white ponies and shoveling their feces wherever they decided to drop it. It was these menial jobs they should have seen coming, collecting and counting plastic rings and darts, scavenging for candy wrappers and balloon remnants and empty bottles of beer, dumping waste—both animal and human—into the nearest woods.

"Shit," Bill said one day while they ate. "There is an awful lot of shit. And cigarette butts."

"Imagine what they're saying at school," Steve said. He ate with enthusiasm, as though on vacation or at camp. Reyna noticed for the first time how wide apart his eyes seemed when he dreamed. "If they could see us now."

The carnival cameraman passed and Steve jumped from his seat. At every opportunity Steve harassed the balding, middle-aged man into taking a picture of the three of them. The cameraman saw Steve and ducked away. He spent his days photographing people but seemed to like none of them.

Bill shook his head at Steve. He looked at Reyna and dropped his face into a mimicking scowl of the cameraman. "Shay cheese goddamnitall."

Reyna smiled. Steve returned with the cameraman and directed him over Bill's shoulder. The cameraman sighed, knowing that taking the picture would be his fastest exit.

Steve sat not in front of his plate but next to Reyna, across from Bill. He placed his arm around Reyna's waist, near her lap. His fingers never came to rest.

Worse than manure detail was scrubbing down hides. Sometime in their second week, on a three-day stop in Dubuque, one of the ponies nearly kicked Steve square in the nose, missing only inches to the left. The hoof gashed Steve's cheek in an upright curve. After seeing the cut, the streaks of blood that turned from purple to red to brown on Steve's face, and the frayed, dirtied bandages they used to conceal it, Reyna nearly fled. Of course, Steve wore the bandage and, eventually, the healing wound proudly, as a badge of their adventures. *Nearly took my head off,* he said to anyone who would listen. He touched the crimson scarring skin to remind them it was still there. *Feisty girl, that one.*

The teenage girl behind the cashier's desk wears a Gifted List apron, as though she is a baker or a coffee shop barista. She has five piercings in each ear. She sits on the counter opposite the cash register with legs crossed. Her eyes scan an electronic reader no bigger than a greeting card. When she notices Reyna she sheepishly tucks it away.

"My boss would kill me," she whispers, leaning forward. "But it's just so easy! I have my movies on this thing too."

Reyna doesn't reply. She looks beyond the girl to the small store. Most of the bookshelves run along the outer walls, arranged in genres almost like a movie rental store itself: mystery, thriller, literary, self-help, children's. Romance, Reyna's favorite. Beyond eye-level stacks in the middle of the store, an empty podium and microphone stand in front of multicolored couches and rows of folding chairs. Many seats are already occupied, a smiling and chattering audience-in-waiting. They hold their copies of his book like trophies.

"The reading," the girl says, noticing Reyna's eyes. She jumps from the counter and pulls a flyer from a small stack. "Just about to start. Suzie landed a big fish tonight. You read Bill Armstrong?"

"Bill," Reyna repeats, the name fighting its way from her mouth. It has been forty years since she's said it. "Bill."

The girl puts a hand on her hip. "It's the new YA craze. My kid sister won't shut up about it. It's like number five on Amazon right now."

Reyna stays silent, not letting on that she doesn't know what *number five on Amazon* means, that she still doesn't own a television or a computer, that she purchased her first cellphone just six months ago.

"Don't tell me you never heard of Colette Clowning."

Reyna looks at the flyer, its top half consumed by the colorful cover of the book: the red-striped carnival tent, the yellows and greens and blues of the various games, the bold, shadowed black title proudly displaying her pseudonym. Tucked in the lower corner is a picture of Bill. His hair still curls, though he has cropped it shorter. He almost smiles. He has the short graying beard and glasses of an author. He looks happy.

Reyna smiles at the teenager. "Yes. It sounds familiar."

Reyna was working the Fantasmic Funhouse the night Bill slogged by with his hand pouring blood. He held it out in front of him, eyeing his pooling palm like a child with a newly won stuffed animal. He seemed to be in no hurry.

Reyna liked working the Funhouse. It was a popular attraction, only costing a nickel. Unlike many of the rigged games—Milk Bottle and Ring Toss were the worst—kids always came out the other end jubilant. And unlike anything bestial, this was clean. Though she'd never been inside, Reyna liked to look at herself in the one mirror tacked to the outer wall. It bulged outward at its center, giving her a plump, watermelon physique beneath a tiny head. The image reminded her of her mother.

Bill didn't look up as he passed. Reyna rushed from her stool and followed him to the farthest tent, where they found the animal doctor sleeping awkwardly in a metal foldout chair, a tipped bottle of whiskey at his side. Bill's lips were pallid. He held his palm up to her. Beneath a veil of blood, right below the thumb, a hole cut straight through to the other side.

"Damn kid threw," he said, his hand quivering, "before I could say go."

So Reyna doused Bill's hand with the whiskey and covered it with equine wrap. It doubled the size of his hand, leaving only his two smallest fingers exposed. Still, spots of bright red blood seeped through to the outermost layers.

Reyna looked up at Bill, who watched not his hand but her.

"Your eyes are deep brown," he said. "Beautiful. How didn't I know that?"

Reyna lowered the hand to Bill's side. The doctor snored and twisted in his chair. Soon he would topple over.

"Do you ever miss home?" Reyna asked.

Bill reclined. "Sure. But when I was home, all I wanted was out. Hit the road. See the world, you know." He shrugged. "Not a whole lot of options for that where we were."

Bill wasn't looking at Reyna now but beyond her, to the clear picture of his life. Reyna tried to do the same but saw nothing but a black, empty screen. Why couldn't Reyna see her own picture? Why couldn't she look with that same straight, determined stare into the future?

"You okay C.C.?" Bill lifted his bandaged hand to Reyna's face. The wrap abraded her cheek. She'd grown to hate the sound of her alias coming from Bill's mouth. Not *Reyna*, not even *Rey*. Even Steve had stopped pondering what their classmates might be saying about them. They had reached Des Moines, not too far but not close. Her past was fast becoming a secret that she would have to keep, alone.

Bill immediately confirmed this: "No, our lives are here." He lifted the hand with pride. "Besides, how could we miss out on all the fun?"

From the podium the Gifted List owner delivers Bill's introduction, which is unabashed: she proclaims words like *revolutionary* and *genius* with flair. She compares Bill favorably to J.K. Rowling. Reyna imagines a young Bill listening to her—to the script his life would become—with a droll, knowing smile on his face.

Then the real Bill emerges from one of the front seats. Reyna hadn't even noticed him. He shuffles half-backward toward the podium, arms waving in thanks for the crowd's liberal applause. He looks much like the picture on the flyer, with slim writer's glasses and trimmed beard. He has embraced his old age in the same way he embraced the inquisitive flair of adolescence: as the obvious next step, as the logical scene to follow. He thanks individual crowd members with his unwavering eyes. He is impressively in the moment.

When he reaches the podium, he places his hand on the owner's back and ushers her aside, as if to say, *I'll take it from here*. The same gentle push, the same paternal smile. Reyna feels the hand on her own back, as though the years and years since she'd last felt it could be erased with just such a gesture: a gentle push, a single step.

He entered her tent on a night in Omaha, somewhere in their second month. Reyna had expected him sooner. In the weeks before his stares had lengthened, had grown deep with the pain of desire. His touches had lingered.

"Well well," Steve said, as though this moment were the culmination of some drawn-out inevitability. Reyna remained silent. The light from campfires projected a flickering blue onto Steve's body as he reached over his head and pulled off his shirt. Then his belt, his pants, until he was naked except for red double-ringed socks. The scar on his face glinted. His chest sunk inward. Reyna had never before noticed how skinny he was.

Through it all Steve was oddly tender, affectionate in the way he cradled his palm under the nape of her neck, in the brief, flighty kisses he landed along her shoulders. He didn't know what he was doing and finished quickly. After, he nestled his head against Reyna's side and started talking. But instead of the words Reyna expected to hear, words of regret or, worse, complicity—*We can't do this anymore*, or *What do we do about Bill?*—he spoke of his childhood, his raving father, his tireless, obedient mother. Reyna heard not the words as much as the soft monotone of Steve's voice, the low, constant hum of it like the large fans used to cool the animals. He talked and talked and talked. His voice lulled her to sleep, and in the morning, Steve was gone.

As he reads, Bill exudes charm. His voice melts from him like a movie narrator. He can look up whenever he wants and never lose his place. It's clear he's read his book, and this particular section of it, many times before. He also does voices. His Steve is incredibly, almost impossibly adept: the soft vowels, the deep guttural j's and g's, the rise at the end of sentences. When speaking as the pony ride attendant he twirls an imaginary, oversized mustache. His cameraman still says *Shay cheese goddamnitall* and gets a laugh from the audience. But for some reason, his Colette Clowning is soft, throaty, overly fragile. Nothing like Reyna's voice. Almost as though, even after decades, Bill feels the need to protect her.

Or perhaps it's because the story he reads now, and likely the entire book, never happened. In the scene, C.C. has discovered an antiquated treasure map near the Carolina coast. When she reveals the map to Bill and Steve—her *Mischievous Men*—they abscond to uncover its purported crates of gold. The book jacket details other adventures, including mimes, hoops of fire and steer-stealing bandits. Reyna smiles. This is why he has succeeded so soundly: as always, Bill's imagination has exceeded his reality.

Then suddenly, right into Bill's perfect reading, right inside a moment where C.C. dodges the cowcatcher of a speeding train, a phone rings. Its tinny bells stop Bill. Reyna stares into the crowd for a moment before realizing the phone is hers. She looks up but it's too late: Bill is staring directly at her.

She shoves her hand into her purse. On the phone's screen, a picture of her son's thirty-something face leers at her with a stupid, cheeks-wide grin. She hates the picture of him, his eyes too far apart, his nose aquiline. His spread arms intend to occupy the entire screen, the entire world. He reminds her too much of his father. The phone rings and rings. The audience turns to her with scowling, scornful eyes. Reyna looks to them, to Bill, to the phone. She doesn't want to answer it, but doesn't know how to silence it. She just wants it to stop ringing.

When it does—her son's face replaced with blue screen and *One Missed Call, 8:07 PM, Junior*—she looks up. Some eyes in the crowd linger to ensure she's registered their anger. At the podium, Bill still stares. He is motionless. The crowd must think that the phone has knocked the master from his footing, has cut the movie reel. He stares so blankly that no one could know he recognizes her.

But then he snaps back with a visible shake of his head. His eyes ungloss.

"Modern technology," he says. He raises his copy of the book. "Back to simpler times."

But a thin undercurrent now stirs his performance. When he looks up, his eyes land only on her. His grip on character voices slackens. He's no longer interested in telling his story and the audience senses it. Likely they blame her interruption: just an anonymous, unthinkable rudeness toward an esteemed author. They would do well to remember the first Bill, the captivating one. The one without her.

It took Reyna four nights. On the first she didn't even pack her bag. The second, she stepped only a few feet from her tent. The third, she reached the edge of camp before turning back. She started to wonder why this— the running home—was harder than running away.

On the fourth night she lay on her back, the moonlight shadow of trees casting twisted arms and fingers across the roof of her tent, her packed bag against her leg. She imagined herself outside her own body: she became an audience member in a great movie hall, watching this young C.C. dumbly stare and assess her own fate. *What are you going back to?* she heard the crowd yammer at the screen. It was a simple, honest question. And the answer: a villainous mother always around, always sitting slovenly in the same overstuffed armchair, always angry. The same three muumuus. The commanding, the yelling. The boyfriends who ran out of money, who tired of her fast. Who eyed young Reyna with contemptible intentions.

But there were moments this audience hadn't seen: her mother buying Reyna a new dress for no reason, or teaching her chopsticks on the piano. The time she saw Reyna nearly in tears holding a feral kitten, then fed it fresh tuna for a week. There were times when her mother wanted nothing more than to touch Reyna's wrist and listen to Frankie Vallie and cry. There were times when her mother's nicotine and wet carpet smell calmed Reyna like nothing else could.

Of course, there were the other times, like the night before they ran away, when Reyna's mother bruised that very wrist simply because Reyna refused to launder their dirty clothes. Reyna recoiled and flung her fist into her mother's side, just below the ribs. The punch stole her mother's breath. She looked at Reyna with the helpless eyes of a child. But Reyna saw past those eyes, to the recalcitrant epicenter of pain her mother kept hidden inside. She saw the truth.

So no, she informed her audience. She wouldn't return to the same mother. The same life. Her stomach groaned and a soft, sweet taste struck her mouth. She touched the stomach, the small downy hairs beneath her belly button. There would be new rules now. She would be starting over.

She stepped from her tent to a cold, starlit night. Somewhere far behind her, two ponies whinnied in conversation. She hoisted her bag and walked.

She stopped only once, at Bill and Steve's tent. She peeked in. They were wrapped under the same blanket, lying head-to-toe, deep in sleep.

What if you had another reason to go back? she would ask Bill. *A new reason. One you never thought you would.* But she could never ask. It was her secret, and hers alone.

Still, she would miss them. Neither would come back for her, enamored as they were of the lifestyle they had created. Neither was ready to cut their picture short of some imagined, marvelous conclusion. She watched their chests rise in unison and realized she could never see them again. Steve was no father; and Bill, honorable, tender, aloof Bill. He would never understand. She pulled her head back out and sucked in night air. She knew she had to go.

Could you run away from running away? Was running home like doing nothing at all?

But Reyna knew, somehow, that it wasn't. That instead of undoing, she was somehow doing double. To her audience it would seem an abrupt end to her short, unfortunate picture. She placed her hand on her quelling stomach, knowing instead that it was a beginning.

Bill pilots the Q & A with authorial aplomb, answering everything just the way the audience wants to hear it. No, he didn't expect the book to be this well-received. Yes and no, the events are inspired by his life, but not necessarily true, in the basic sense of the word. Yes, he knew the ending before he began: that although she enjoyed the life, although she seemed to have everything she needed, C.C. would run back home. The only question that draws a laugh from Bill is, *When's the movie coming out?* He nods and shrugs. "I'd be lying if I said I hadn't thought about it." His eyes turn to Reyna. "Casting would be tough. I can't see anyone as Colette. A young Grace Kelly maybe."

Reyna watches the book signing from behind the travel stacks. Bill smiles, asks names, swipes a ballpoint across the title page and, whenever one runs dry, deftly retrieves another. His hand never tires. He was always sweet in those quick doses, like hard candy. But every so often his eyes rise to the gradually shortening line ahead of him, beyond the crowds, into the shadowed recesses of the store. The eyes are expectant. Waiting for his C.C. to appear again like a dove from a hat. Just like that: like magic.

And in that moment, Reyna finally sees her movie playing out, reel by glorious reel. She drops his book with a soft smack on the table, startling him to attention. He looks up and smiles all at once. His eyes grow young. His overworked hand reaches out to hers, but when he sees the line behind her, when he remembers the man he has become, the hand stops. He reassumes his act.

"And to whom should I make this out?" he asks.

"An old friend."

His fingers graze her wrist as he hands back the book. His smile for the next woman in line is so large she flushes as red as her curled hair. The woman now has her own story, one to tell friends for years.

His signature in Reyna's book is brief but beautifully written, his script graceful, almost womanly. It includes a hotel and room number.

Before she can even knock he opens the door. He has bought flowers, a bouquet of particolored roses, yellow and purple and orange and red. He places the *Do Not Disturb* tag on the door before closing it.

Bill pours two glasses of wine but doesn't touch his. He is no longer the charmer: he rubs his hands at the pockets of his slacks, exhales and softly laughs when he tries to speak. Reyna sits at the edge of the bed like a teenager as Bill half-moons around her. He moves closer with hesitation, as though dipping his toes into the voluminous ocean of their shared past.

And then—because this is Reyna's movie—she dives in head-first and lets all the words cascade out. Like a clown's never-ending handkerchief, she spills the years between them, the pain of leaving, the dry sundrenched days, the moonless nights. The yearning, day after day, to return to that night outside their tent, to wake Bill and divulge everything. To tell him she was sorry. They press their tearstained cheeks together, this pained union somehow channeling the ocean of everything that could have been into a clear, flowing river of what could be.

But then the red-haired woman waylays Bill, her hardcover copy of his book in her hand and a child's smile on her face. She prattles so loudly her voice engulfs the entire store. And Bill's blinking eyes shutter over Reyna's brilliant film, cutting it abruptly. He is—has been and will continue to be, from this reel on—the wonderfully amicable author who will still give this chipper woman her minute. Reyna turns from them and leaves the travel section. She exits Gifted List through the back, into an alleyway where the teenage worker smokes a cigarette with her back against the building. The girl looks up only for a moment, her eyes deep in some thought, some dream of times to come, some film as of yet unscripted.

White Lies

It seems the sedan will stop backing at any moment. The fire-red flash of brake lights, the rocking momentum shift, the tire squeal. One of those jarring narrow misses, a stomach-in-the-throat close call that jolts a driver to attention but is then soon forgotten. But the sedan doesn't stop. If anything it speeds up. Its driver, a goateed, middle-aged man in a baseball hat—he looks like an Evan, or an Eric—apparently has little interest in his car's trajectory, including the elderly woman with a walker inching behind him at a cross angle. The woman, an Ethel, moves but not quickly enough. She wears a blue tunic dress, bifocals, corkscrews of white hair and a wincing face. Midway through the crosswalk she notices the car and, in the way of someone who knows the speeds at which she can and cannot move, just keeps on her path. Eric does the same. Midway through the crosswalk Ethel finally stops, dead in the car's path. Eric is going fast, faster than anyone should in reverse. Ethel glances around the sparse lot. She shrugs to no one, then hoists her walker and hurls its tennis-balled end directly into Eric's bumper.

The red lights finally ignite. The car stops.

From his own sedan in the next row, David absorbs it all with detached wonder. He was out for a simple cup of coffee—his longtime girlfriend Lily has become oddly forgetful with groceries as of late—and was buckling his seatbelt when he first saw Eric, Ethel, the strange and hazardous collision path they'd engendered. David had almost shouted, which would have done nothing. He might have laid on his horn but the thought hadn't occurred to him. Now, the incident over, he feels the urge to applaud Ethel, right there in his car, even if she won't hear.

But he is wrong; the incident is not over. Eric springs from his car. He is short, his goatee thick and forearm veins visible. He runs to the back of his car, ignoring Ethel in lieu of his bumper. He lays a careful finger across its entirety before grabbing Ethel's walker and slamming it into the pavement.

David shakes at the rattling noise, at Eric's incorrigible shouts that follow. Eric berates Ethel just inches from her face, his saliva flecking her glasses. He allows her no opportunity to speak. When she attempts to hobble to her walker he cuts her off. He raises a hand in the air, looking as though he will bring it down on her head.

David scans the parking lot, waiting for someone to do what he knows must be done. But no one else is around. He watches this man—who nearly struck an elderly woman with his car, now about to do so with his fist— and it all feels distant, disembodied, as though his windshield is a television screen tuned to some bad reality show. As though, even if he did enter the scene, they wouldn't acknowledge him.

Ethel finally retrieves her walker. She shuffles away in the opposite direction she'd been heading. Eric wants to follow her but restrains himself, though he continues yelling at her back before examining his bumper a final time. He pulls out his cellphone and returns to the driver's seat. With phone in hand he leaves the lot, undoubtedly recounting to someone a brutishly flawed version of the events David just witnessed.

David watches Ethel plod down the sidewalk, her head hung, her intended destination seemingly lost. He waits five minutes, maybe more, until Ethel clears from sight, before starting his car.

Lily doesn't look up when David enters. Her attention is buried in her plate of eggs and tablet on the table. She wears a lime green tracksuit, her hair in a ponytail. David idles in the doorway for half a minute, coffee long since cold in his hand, as she scoops bites with one hand and scrolls internet articles with the other.

She finally finishes, dabs at the corners of her mouth with a napkin. Then she looks up. Her eyes squint. "What's wrong with you?"

In her tone resides, not an accusation exactly, but certainly a hint of exasperation. Of wondering what David did wrong this time. In their two years together, Lily has seen him gain and then lose three mediocre paralegal positions and is accustomed to his periodic, apathetic failures. So he begins the story. The car, the walker, the awkward collision course. But after a few sentences he loses grip of the narrative. He finds its particulars elusive, transient. He's altogether more shaken than he expected, circumstances considered. He stutters and backtracks; he intermixes his current thoughts with the event itself; he calls the man Eric and has to explain why; he so bumbles over the heart of the matter— "So he throws the thing to the ground! And she's... No, wait..."—that Lily's apparent disdain becomes concern. She stands, comes to his side. When he reaches the height of Eric's anger, she touches his forearm with delicate conviction. The feel of her fingertips centers him. He starts over, at the moment Eric accosts Ethel, ready to give a clearer testimony.

But things only get hazier. With Lily's hand on him, caressing as he recounts, David finds himself exaggerating Eric's facial features, his goatee curled, his brow inhumanly angled. Ethel reels more, her body quivering under its own weight. He reaches the crucial moment, Eric's hand raised to strike, and suddenly, quite naturally, instead looking around for others, David abounds from his own car. He approaches the two with valiant poise.

Hitting a stride, the story itself convalesces in his mind, solidifies. Like a director's reshoot, something in his mind calls out, *Yes, this is the one.* Before he realizes it, David has told Lily everything that should have happened: him over-shouting Eric with threats to call the police, Eric stomping away in defeat, Ethel inundating David with appreciation. After making sure Ethel is uninjured, as others make their way to the scene, David returns promptly to his car because, after all, he hadn't done it for praise. He just wanted to help.

David finally stops. Lily exhales as though she's been holding her breath. She shakes her head. "People are unbelievable!" she says, decrying the devil-like image of Eric that David has created. But she quickly softens, and rests her body against his. Her newfound pride in him radiates from her, tangible as the warmth of her skin.

"I can't believe it," she says softly, close enough to a whisper that David almost misses it. "I can't believe you did that."

♦ ♦ ♦

David assumes that—after a day or two, a week tops—his fabricated heroism will fall, like so many minor episodes, into the annals of forgotten memory. A little white lie, a spore among many upon the windswept dandelion of life. He expects Lily will stop talking about it. Instead the incident seems to billow, cloud-like, into something that hangs over their entire lives. She demands he retell the story to her at meals, to her Marquette law school colleagues at their weekly night out, to her mother over the phone. He tells it two, three times a day, so many that not only the moments but the sentences themselves harden, become resolute. *And the goateed guy, he showed no signs of slowing down... I know! Right at his speeding bumper!... So what else could I do?* Each new audience presents varying degrees of praise, but always an excessive amount from Lily. *That poor woman was just so lucky... We need more people like Dave.* And each compliment, a lie in itself, piles atop the real David who did, not the wrong thing, but nothing. Not the perpetrator, but the Bad Samaritan. A month later, after a particularly effusive night with David's softball team, as they reclaim their sides of the bed, as Lily softly snores beside him, he tries to remind himself there's a difference.

Six months later, resting comfortably on Lily's father's pontoon during a weekend getaway to the Hahn family lake home, imported beer in hand and sun on his face, in a moment of brilliant clarity, David finally realizes the reason for Lily's infatuation. He'd been so preoccupied with the story, with his lie and the imminent challenge of living it, that he missed all the obvious signs. All the clues so masqueraded to him at the time unveil themselves: the slow dwindling of food, the late nights at the library. The gradual excising of her wardrobe in their shared closet. Of course. Lily had planned to leave him.

Lily's father Herb asks David to take the helm while he helps himself to the cooler. He fills a glass with four fingers of bourbon and two ice cubes. He lights a stocky cigar, scratches at his graying chest hair with a strange affection. Herb has always struck David as a man who enjoys the impression of himself—the bourbon, the cigar, the chest hair—even when there is no one around to impress. Who lives as though the world is watching him and universally approves. He smiles away from the boat, at nothing in particular, his cheeks shining a glistening, alcohol-infused red.

Behind the jetblack steering wheel David finishes his beer. He knows the realization that his girlfriend intended to leave him just months earlier should sink his spirits, but instead it buoys him. He calls back to Herb for a bourbon of his own. Herb looks to David, then to his wife Lucia, then Lily. He fishes another glass and pours the bourbon with what David can only describe as pride. As he hands David the glass, he tells him to stay put right there in the captain's chair. He joins Lucia in the back seats under the shade. She settles into his arm, the experience of his affections on the water clearly atypical. He glances over and salutes David with glass in hand, as though David has just now, this very instant, become the type of person he wishes to invite aboard. As though the family Hahn is an exclusive club to which he has just now gained membership.

That night, in their small kitchen, drunk on bourbon and sun, David asks Lily to marry him. He offers his deceased grandmother's quarter-carrot ring he had, before this moment, no intention of giving away. They make love on the sofa. Though it's nearly one in the morning, Lily calls Lucia and Herb, who lightheartedly chastise David for not proposing on the boat, in their presence.

In the coming months, their discussions turn to floral arrangements, guest lists. The River Hills Golf Club or the Hilton, DJ or cover band. The Caribbean immediately after. Talk of the wedding, thankfully, subsumes talk of the incident. David goes days without thinking of it. He becomes confident that, after a long enough time—post-wedding perhaps—the incident will finally be put out to sea, will become jetsam that rarely, if ever, drifts ashore.

The rehearsal dinner at the Pfister Hotel is lavish and spectacular: silk linens and chair covers, white freesias and roses and peonies bursting from vases like inverted chandeliers, pepper-crusted filet mignon and Maine lobster in the buffet line. A four-piece string quartet in tuxedos and black dresses. Herb has opened both his pocketbook and personality with gusto. He greets guests like a politician, firmly accepting handshakes and congratulations. David lingers near the bar, ordering Herb a bourbon whenever his gets low, drinking his own nearly as fast. He has come to like the drink, to like the look he receives when ordering one.

Their guests eat heartily, chewing and conversing, filling plates two at a time. Tines scrape and glasses clink. Two young girls—Lily's nieces, David can't remember their names—swerve and hum around the tables like go-carts. The combination of class and chaos, David finds, suits him well. He reaches for Lily's hand. She turns to him, breaking her conversation with Lucia. She smiles, squeezes his hand, and stands.

"Thank you thank you thank you," she calls into the cacophony. The violin players recognize and abruptly cut short their Tchaikovsky. One of them brings Lily a microphone as attention seeps her way. "Thank you all so much for being here. This is truly amazing." From a back table someone shouts "You're damn right!" and everyone chuckles. Lily continues through the formalities: a loving personal message to each of her six bridesmaid sisters, like Lily all named after flowers; gratitude for those who needed to travel; extra gratitude to her parents for fronting the bill. David sips the dregs of his drink, eyeing the preposterously expensive silverware through the bottom of his glass. Then Lily puts her hand on his shoulder. "Stand up with me, Dave. This is your night too."

So he does, though he plans nothing more than to reiterate what Lily has already offered, to extend a formal ditto. But she continues: "As you all know, Dave and I have been dating for a while. But they say there's always a moment when you realize—when it hits you, and you think, You know what? I'm going to marry this man."

David's body seizes. The sweet taste of bile, of bourbon and steak, floods his mouth.

"It was just this random Saturday. I was in the kitchen..."

And, like lighting, the story strikes. Lily not only recalls the incident, she delivers a stout, heartfelt oration better than any before it. She pauses at heightened moments, collapses her index fingers toward one another in simulation. She shines. "And then, just when this maniac seems like he's about to actually strike this poor woman," she narrates, stoic but with latent gratification ready to burst forth. She will make, David realizes, a remarkable trial lawyer.

But then, just before she delivers the next moment, the first outright perjury leading to all the others, she pauses to slip her arm from his. She looks in his eyes. Their faces feel unnaturally close. And for the briefest second—so quick David can't even be certain of it—a hint of something irregular, something vindictive even, enters her eyes. She turns back to her rapt audience. "This man next to me, my soon-to-be husband, he gets out of his car."

David turns away from Lily to the crowd. Does she know? And for how long? As she continues, David recognizes the possibility. The probability even. The David she had known up to that point—the true David— had proven himself time and again a coward, a non-committer. The last one to act. At a distant table, his second-cousin Charlie shoots him two thumbs-up. Lily's great-aunt Gertrude, or Ginny, or some old G-name he can't remember, shifts her eyes from Lily to David and back as though watching a tennis match. And David recognizes the thin, sensational veil that is Lily's speech. The look in her eye, this entire charade, is a challenge. A call to confess.

"And you wouldn't believe it." She pauses, her hands extended like a priest's. "But David shouts this devious man away."

It makes all too much sense. Months of her summoning the story at inappropriate times, with friends old and new, with service workers at restaurants, with strangers in elevators. After all, what he'd done—what he'd invented to do—wasn't so heroic anyway, at least not to the degree she now presents it, in front of the seventy-plus people they hold in highest regard. David suddenly notices a rift in the audience: just beside them, two of Lily's sisters snicker and share whispered secrets. Do they know too? Has Lily gossiped about David's duplicity before? When her uncle calls out "Brave man," David perceives a hint of sarcasm in his tone. It seems cruel, downright dastardly, for Lily to corner David this way, to attempt to force an avowal on the largest scale possible, in front of many people whose very impression and good standing of David reside in the lie itself. To pull the collective wool from the eyes of those who comprise the locus of David's world. It feels like some twisted intervention.

David visibly sweats. He loosens his tie. Just as the nausea threatens to overpower him, Lily finally finishes with a wistful "And that's when I knew." The applause is suspiciously light. Without looking at David, Lily says: "Anything you'd like to add honey?"

The question is innocuous enough, but David feels the underlying tones of a threat. "I—" he begins, but gets nowhere after. He feels the heat of the room's attention on him. Herb stares right at David, his body issuing a nonverbal challenge. Next to him, Lucia dispels a dry cough. Even his groomsmen, six assorted friends split evenly between high school and college, share shifty glances.

But then the microphone is wrested from his hand by an unlikely source: Lily's sister Jasmine. The quiet one, the black sheep. The only bridesmaid to forego a dress and wear her hair in a simple bun. "I think," she says, placing a pacifying hand on David's shoulder, "as usual, my sister has said it all."

She raises her champagne glass. The guests follow her lead. Lily clinks hers against David's, though she looks down at the table. The low strums of the cellist rush into the room. The party continues.

For the rest of the evening, Lily's speech bleeds onto everything. He tries to accept congratulations, well-wishes, light-hearted jibes, but he can only see Ethel shrugging, her walker banging against the bumper, Eric accosting her, and all the while his whole body locked. Not a single motion, not even a shift in his seat or hand off his wheel. He tries various times to gain Lily's attention, but she pinballs across the room from guest to guest, adorning each one with her unflagging attention.

Near the exit, Jasmine cloaks her shoulders in a secondhand sweater. David approaches and thanks her for saving him.

"We all know Lily," she says. "Everything's this massive deal. Takes after Dad that way." She accepts the hand of the young man beside her, a stick-thin kid with gauged earlobes. "Hell," she says, laughing, as though the thought has just come to her, "you're the one who has to live with her the rest of your life."

"Yeah," David says. And then Jasmine is gone.

Around sundown the remainder of the guests wander out in small flocks. The bartender shuts the taps. And eventually Lily finds her way back to him. She slides into him, rests her head in the hollow between his shoulder and chest. The warmth of her body startles him. She continues to entertain, giving sarcastic warnings about bedtimes and wake-up calls. He pulls her closer and she accepts.

And suddenly it dawns on him, how unlikely, impossible even, that Lily has known the entire time. That she would go to such lengths—an engagement! a lavish rehearsal dinner!—just to suss him out. The punishment in no way fits the crime. She finally brings her eyes to his, and he searches for the tinge of hostility, the challenge, whatever had appeared there during her speech. He finds nothing.

◆ ◆ ◆

The third day of their honeymoon, on the Honduran
island of Roatán, they lay on oversized towels along their
resort's beach. The sun is high and unforgiving, the water
profusely blue. Each day has become progressively rum-
soaked, syrupy, the hours melting together. They have
plans later to snorkel over a sunken shipwreck. David
knows, with Lily's third strawberry daiquiri on the way,
that they may not make it. He doesn't much mind.

They lunch at the resort café and decide to go anyway.
Before David knows it he's out of his swimsuit and into
his perpetually damp island clothes: a loose-fitting
button-down shirt, khaki shorts, sunglasses strapped
about his neck. He enjoys playing the tourist. Lily dresses
more local, flowing skirts and tops bought greedily on
their first day. Today she succeeds a bit more in her
impersonation, or perhaps the drink is simply settling
in, the façade easier on the palate.

Like the days before, they rent a power scooter from
one of the many island men named Loren just outside
their resort. Seeing them approach, Loren pulls what has
become their scooter—a navy blue number with orange
lightning bolts down its side—and exchanges the keys
for cash with enthusiasm. He showers Spanish
compliments upon Lily that she doesn't understand but
still make her blush. They thank Loren, adorn their
rented helmets and set off.

They pass sights now familiar: an abandoned adobe
convenience store, the cruise ship quay, a field littered
with palm fronds. The briny wind seeps into David's
nostrils. "You know where this thing is?" he asks over
his shoulder, but Lily doesn't hear. The island is small,
and they ride out with every expectation that, eventually,

they will discover their destination. As of yet it hasn't failed them.

So David pulls back on the gas to take in the sights around him. What a discordant amalgam of worlds Roatán held: new money amidst old-world charm, pockets of touristy luxury juxtaposed against supreme poverty. He estimates fifty cars tops on the island, and many of them broken down. They approach the one traffic light on the entire island, near the quay, its glimmering green almost futuristic against the natural flora surrounding it.

But then he sees a white Lexus in front of them, completely out of place and going way too fast, and *déjà vu* lambasts him. Ahead of the Lexus, a rusted-out truck awaits a left turn behind a group of tourists. The Lexus doesn't slow, doesn't seem like it will or even could. David stops, grounds his feet. He waits for the red flash of brake lights, the rocking shift of momentum. For the Lexus to swerve, to narrowly miss, to blow through the intersection startled but unharmed.

"What—" Lily says, but she's cut off by the shrieking sound of metal on metal. The Lexus stops dead, like a cue ball, but sends the truck careening at the tourists. They shout and scatter. The truck veers just enough to shoot the gap between fleers and crashes into a palm tree.

The pedestrians quickly examine themselves and each other. The truck driver, a local likely named Loren, stumbles out his concaved door, hand on his head. A teenager in a baseball hat, his brusque voice eerily reminiscent of Eric, frantically scans his family, his shouts of "Are you okay?" rising above the commotion. Then this younger Eric turns, his body a flailing jumble of anger, and runs at Loren. Loren looks up in a daze; before he knows it, this Eric shoves him into his own truck, pinning him against the side of the bed. Eric's shouts are earsplitting and incoherent.

All the attention focuses on these two, on Eric fighting his instinct to thrash Loren. A female relation of Eric pleads but does nothing to really stop him. David turns back to the road, where the real perpetrator in the Lexus flickers his lights and lurches forward, as though testing his ability. It seems impossible that the scoundrel will simply escape. But there go his wheels, slowly turning as he creeps through the intersection.

The scooter teeters beneath David; he just catches it. He turns but Lily is no longer there. She has stepped some distance away from him, her body slack and face aghast. Her eyes flash to his, and a strange surge of heat rises to his chest. He turns back to the scene, watches Eric's misplaced anger cascade out, listens as his young screams populate the sky. Then David looks at his own hands, still on the scooter and tremoring with the engine's low purr as he wills them, and wills them, to let go.

Encyclopedia Alanica

A lan: (Irish, "Handsome, Peaceful") 21 August 1987–
Present. Of Kimberly, Wisconsin, born and raised.
Man of medium height (5'11" at last doctor's visit) and
slightly above-average weight (204 pounds, same visit).
Married five years to Hailey Mosley, also of Kimberly.
Employed by Kimberly Parks and Street Department. Job
Title: Street Patch and Repair Crew. Post-high-school,
three-and-a-half-semester attendant of University of
Wisconsin-Stevens Point (tenure relatively long in
comparison to majority of Kimberly High School
graduates) and four weeks attendant of Fox Valley
Technical College: no degrees earned. At present (see also
Today), eating Roundy's microwaveable breakfast bagel,
comprised of egg, sausage, and yellow sauce that must be
some sort of hollandaise, contemplating approximate
amount of eleven-pound weight gain attributable to
switch, made three months previous, from bowl of whole
grain cereal, this contemplation being the first of many
incidents throughout typical day in which Alan considers,
catalogues, and ultimately overanalyzes his own behavior
(see *Alan's Dominant Behaviors and Traits*).

Kimberly, Wisconsin: 1889–Present. Founded by John A. Kimberly, cofounder of paper company Kimberly-Clarke. Located at 44°16'6"N, 88°20'15"W, Wisconsin, United States of America. Small-to-mid village of approximately 15,400 people (2010 Census). Current graduating high school class of 257. Distance from northeast to southwest corner Hailey once claimed to have driven in 1'21" logistically calling for one of three scenarios:

1. multiple instances of posted speed limit and/ or stop sign disobedience,
2. extreme exaggeration by Hailey (see *Hailey's Dominant Behaviors and Traits*), or
3. both.

Today: 5 July 2017 (see also *The Present*).

Hailey: (Scandinavian, "Heroine") 29 January 1989–Present. Of Kimberly, Wisconsin, raised, not born. Woman of distinct natural beauty, mainly in curl of blonde hair and fair complexion. Two-time runner-up in local beauty pageants (Miss Teen Appleton 2006, Miss Fox Valley 2009), zero-time winner. At present, in kitchen, standing across from Alan, watching toaster brown and then slightly blacken morning toast, opened jar of bleu cheese-stuffed green olives in right hand, jabbing fork in left, removing and eating olives two-by-two, to this point fourteen by Alan's estimation.

Yesterday was fun: Words spoken by Hailey in direction of the refrigerator, near but not to Alan, linguistically disguised as a statement but, through inflection on last word, sounding more like a rhetorical question, one of

Hailey's common speech patterns which, in theory, would seem to invite response but actually shuts down communication, at least for Alan.

Weak Nod: (see *Non-Verbal Communications*) Alan's go-to response.

You bringing back the pontoon today?: Question posed from Hailey to table where Alan sits.

Van Zeeland Aquamarine Rentals: Retail rental store at 124 North Railroad Avenue, directly across from Excel Auto Parts Store and cattycorner from McDonald's. Owned by George Van Zeeland, father of Darren Van Zeeland. Specialty: rental of watercrafts, in particular Jet Skis and pontoon boats.

Rental of one pontoon boat, 4 July 2017: Reason why Alan Mosley had initial contact with Van Zeeland Aquamarine Rentals, 129.45 USD rental plus tax paid with debit Mastercard.

Late[1]: (See also *Not on Time, Post-Haste,* and *Beyond Desired Temporal Expectancy*) Alan's future return of pontoon, subject to 25.00 USD fine, as rental agreement expired at 8:00:00 Central Standard Time, 4 July.

Intoxication, mainly via tequila: Reason why he didn't return it on time.

Inability to drive stick shift, inability to back up with trailer hitched to truck, general distrust in self to not hit anything or anyone with said trailer, general

dislike for driving Alan's truck, slight intoxication: Reasons why Hailey didn't return it on time.

Is everything okay with you?: Second question posed from Hailey, this time directly to Alan (see similar entries for 3 and 1 July, 2017, in addition to numerous entries June and May 2017).

The Sound of Silence: Song by folk rock group Simon and Garfunkel, acoustic version first released on album *Wednesday Morning, 3 AM* on 19 October 1964, occasionally aired on Appleton easy-listening, adult-contemporary radio station 94.3 WROE, the station most frequently played in Mosley household, as it is now, as the song is now, its irony not lost on Alan.

Intercostobrachial Nerve: Small space just below underarm where Hailey touches Alan, two fingers directly on skin, two over sleeve of t-shirt.

Similar hand-to-back-of-arm gesture: Exact moment Alan realized his desire to wed Hailey, on a stormy day, May 2011.

Deep, intimate care for Alan's well-being, coupled with slight but desirable pang of dependency: What, to Alan, gesture symbolized.

Rarely: (see also *Seldom, Hardly Ever,* and *Once in a Blue Moon*) How often similar exchanges have occurred between Alan and Hailey in previous three years, an approximately long time in relation to average human life span (+/- 81.5 years), approximately short time in relation to the world (+/- 4,500,000,000 years).

The Past: Vast, haphazardly defined portion of history, typically human, commonly understood—though through speculation only—as main predictor of its counterparts The Present and The Future.

Out of kitchen, into front-door foyer area, past sunken living room, up stairs, past one of two spare bedrooms intended as office/workout room but quickly devolved into dumping ground for clutter, through master bedroom and into master bathroom: Hailey's path immediately after breakfast, repeated 2'37" later by Alan.

August 22, 2015: Closing date on property and house, 600 Stone Gate Drive, Kimberly, Wisconsin, purchased from owner-sellers Will and Elizabeth Mosley by Alan after getting over initial aversion to owning and living in house in which he grew up, mowing lawn on which he'd camped out, sleeping in room in which he was conceived, a surprisingly easy accomplishment, considering.

Shower/shave legs (simultaneous); dry hair; brush teeth; apply makeup (generously), deodorant, lotion on elbows and kneecaps, anti-stretchmark crème on inside and back of thighs, perfume (also generously) on neck, wrists, and chest: Hailey's morning routine— all steps crucial for a hair stylist, Hailey has assured Alan—buzzing around Alan's relatively short routine of inserting contacts, shaving neck, brushing/flossing/ mouthwashing, getting dressed in khakis and Kimberly

Parks and Street Department gray-and-black polo shirt, retrieving Appleton *Post-Crescent* from front porch, rounding up all trashes and dumping into 35-gallon receptacle in garage.

Bedroom Trash, Contents: Three used dryer sheets; empty perfume bottle, impracticably tear-shaped; four dead AAA batteries from television remote; crumpled-up paper towel stained orange, used to clean orange juice spill, night of 3 July 2017.

Bathroom Trash, Contents: Empty mouthwash bottle; two bar-soap boxes; fourteen used Q-Tips, some for removal of ear wax (Alan), most for swabbing of eye makeup (Hailey); fingernail clippings; old sports section of Appleton *Post-Crescent.*

Tampon Wrappers: What have been noticeably absent from bathroom trash for at least three months, observed but not commented on by Alan (avoidance of confrontation one of Alan's Dominant Behaviors and Traits, maybe at top of list, if list were ordered and numbered).

Late[2]: What Hailey possibly is, despite lack of early warning signs (see *Morning Sickness, Hormonal Imbalances* and *Odd Cravings,* among others), despite multiple drinks consumed on pontoon boat 4 July, despite lack of wrappers remaining only tangible evidence for the case, surely not enough to convict.

One American-Flag Bandana[1]: Rather tacky yet highly popular 18"x18" head attire noticeably present in bathroom trash, brown-stained from rum-and-Diet-Coke spill, rolled and tied the way Hailey wears it.

One American-Flag Bandana[2]: What Alan found under the sheets at foot of their guest bed four months previous.

In the garage: Where Alan leaves bedroom and bathroom trash cans, after dumping into curbside receptacle, in concordance with desire to not return upstairs.

Own mailbox, neighbor's mailbox, ditch: What, in order, Alan nearly backs 2002 Ford F-150 (see entry for *Cheap Trucks*) with pontoon trailer still hitched into.

Both red lights on Kimberly Avenue and a train crossing the intersection, reversing, and going forward again in order to switch tracks: Hindrances causing Alan's drive to work to take considerably longer (8'55") than usual (3' to 4').

Pain in the padded ass: Way Alan's grandfather Jack would have described attempts to park Ford F-150/ trailer combination in undersized Kimberly Parks and Street Department parking lot.

Kimberly Parks and Street Department: Established 1927 by Owen Baker (deceased 1958, survived by various grandchildren and great-grandchildren, all of Kimberly). Located at 515 W. Kimberly Avenue. Current employer of eight full-time workers, Alan included, six over 50 years of age (see *Lifers*), Alan not included, and four seasonal summer employees of collegiate age, two competent, two not.

Kimberly Parks and Street Department Garage,
Contents: Six small-sized orange street cones; seventeen
medium-sized orange street cones; sixteen large orange
street barrels; one 1993 Bolens 12.5-Horsepower Manual
38-inch Cut Lawn Tractor; one 2016 John Deere 18.5-
Horsepower Hydrostatic 42-inch Cut Zero Turn Radius
Mower; one John Deere self-propelling push mower;
three metal rakes, two rusted; one industrial-sized broom;
two red 5-gallon gasoline cans, one half-full, one empty;
rubber skid marks on concrete in the form of letters Y
and O; one *Maxim* magazine 2017 "Girls of *Maxim*"
calendar, posted on wall, flipped to July; torn-out and
Scotch-taped pictures from *Maxim* calendar, months
January-June, April a blonde in blue swimsuit with semi-
open mouth and crotch area circled in permanent marker;
analog punch clock; wooden timecard holder mounted
on wall; fourteen timecards, varying amounts of dirt
fingerprints; Gary Warner (see also *Big Werny*); Alan.

You're late again, Mosley: Words spoken from Big
Werny to Alan, punch-in clock noting 3'13" difference
in time required and time actual.

Big Werny: (No known origin) 29 February 1963–
Present. Of Kimberly, Wisconsin, neither born nor
raised. Street Crew boss named ironically for small
stature (5'3" on a good day). Mustache too big for face,
often catching food, like the crumbs of what must now
be a Captain Crunch Crunchberry. Married 23 years,
without children, to Stella Warner, nature of relationship
never shown to be more than platonic excepting public
occasions involving intoxication (see *Kimberly Parks and
Street Department Christmas Bash 2014, Werny's 25-Years-*

With-The-Company Anniversary Party, and *That One Awkward Time in the Break Room*).

<Burp>: Onomatopoeic word for the expelling of extraneous stomach gasses through the mouth Alan does in response to both Big Werny's comment and breakfast bagel settling in stomach.

We shouldn't have to come in the day after the Fourth anyway: What burp may have intended to say or wished to say (see also related entries: *Things Alan should have said, wanted to say, nearly said, would have said if it weren't for some unforeseen circumstance or bad timing, didn't have the balls to say*).

Keep it up, Mosley. Objurgate yourself right outta town: Werny's linguistically unclear but intentionally clear words to Alan.

Objurgate: To criticize; to berate harshly; to express extreme disapproval of actions (see also *Dictionary.com Word of the Day, 5 July 2017*).

Because he's a Leap Baby: Reason why many Street Crew workers, particularly Lifers, characterize Big Werny's oddities and swings in mood as eccentrically endearing.

Sexual Frustration: Complex mixture of disappointment, sadness and seething rage, generally manifested in headaches, tightness of the chest and unsettled groin, that Alan believes causes Werny to be Werny.

Big Werny's Dominant Behaviors and Traits:
Listening to Carly Simon; smoking exactly one-half of
Montecristo cigar daily; getting food lodged into
mustache; finger-gunning camera in photographs;
theatrically commencing useless speeches; calling people
into office to seem important; wearing Hawaiian shirts
when off-duty; online shopping.

Alan Mosley's Work List, 5 July 2017:
    CREW: Alan, Danny, Luke
    1. Replace pothole on southside Kimberly Avenue
    2. Trim and woodchip branches close to power
       lines on Third and Oak
    3. Mow lawn of foreclosed homes:
        a. Looper house on Stone Gate
        b. Van Lieshout house on Second
    4. Start mowing and painting lines on Sunset
       Park diamonds for upcoming fastpitch tourney

Danny driving, Alan shotgun, Luke bitch: How, after
loading bed, crew members fall into truck, quite naturally
and without need of verbal communication.

Kimberly Avenue Shops, North to South End:
Createch Printing Services; Joe's Power Shack, parking
lot filled with boat parts and cars on cinderblocks; Bill
the Barber barbershop, two red-and-blue neck-high
barbershop poles flanking doorway; Milly's Market
Foods; Kimberly Pharmacy, home of the soda fountain,
chocolate-strawberry-banana milkshake, penny arcade
and five-tier magazine rack with pornography
pharmacy store owners constantly shoo adolescent boys
away from.

Stirring pothole gravel mixture and pouring: Not a difficult job but hot, particularly in July, particularly with Luke spending approximately 45 minutes on cellphone texting girlfriend, hometown friends, friends from college, cousins, or anyone who will respond.

Brown 2012 Chevrolet Silverado Extended Cab, orange-and-green Kimberly Parks and Street Department sticker on side: What Werny pulls up in, radio playing Carly Simon's "Nobody Does it Better."

Big Werny out of the office, on site, before lunch: Never a good sign.

See you for a sec, Mosley: Big Werny's address, more statement than question.

Thinly shaved turkey with dash of brown mustard: Food now lodged in Big Werny's mustache, remnant of daily meal between breakfast and lunch (not to be confused with brunch, which may imply Werny skips either breakfast or lunch).

Overly familiar arm on Alan's shoulder; sneaky peek to right and left; conspiratorial head-tilt; fatherly clearing-of-the-throat: Big Werny's theatrical commencement to words (see *Werny's Dominant Behaviors and Traits*) indicating to Alan that out of Werny's mouth will come nothing worthwhile.

I been thinking about how I come down on you. But you know, I get it. It's a job, right? Hey, no kid sits in front of class and says *When I get older, I'm gonna*

paint lines on the goddamn street: Werny's opening, not as inarticulate as expected.

You think I wanted to run this place? Be a Lifer? Shit. I wanted to be Humphrey Bogart. With this mug, can you imagine?: Werny's surprisingly candid admission, one hand pointing at walrus-like jowls on face.

Lifers: Danny, Jer-Ball (nicknamed after first name Jerry and tendency to always carry around brown, weathered baseball in back pocket), Tonnage (or One-Ton, nicknamed after stout, bowling-ball-esque body type), Susan, James, Crazy (nickname self-explanatory) and Big Werny.

But Mosley, I just hope you don't tackle everything the way you tackle a pothole. You know what I'm getting at: Werny's getting-to-the-point, also surprisingly sensible.

Contemplative glance onto Kimberly Avenue: Alan's response.

Alan's Dominant Behaviors and Traits: Avoiding confrontation; considering, cataloging, and ultimately overanalyzing own behavior; drinking Pabst Blue Ribbon from can or Miller Genuine Draft from bottle; stopping speech mid-sentence as though someone has cut him off; house maintenance and upkeep; watching and reading all things Green Bay Packers; wishing he were somewhere else; masturbating to thoughts of own wife; building wooden household contraptions, some useful (see *Bookshelf, Rack for Pots and Pans* and *Basement Pull-Up*

Bar), some not (see *Flower Window Box, Floating Kitchen Island Bar* and *Broken Stepping Stool*); reading historical fiction.

White 2010 Dodge Caravan, triple-blue Van Zeeland Aquamarine Rental logo on side: Vehicle that, in concordance with Alan's shitty luck and/or inability to remain complacent for more than mere moments, drives past as Werny walks away.

Darren: (Irish, "Great") August 15, 1989–Present. Of Kimberly, Wisconsin, born and raised. Man in White 2010 Dodge Caravan (see entry for *Cheap Mini-Vans and SUVs*). Member of Kimberly High School class of 2007; part of group with stitched patches of local bands, horror movies and pot leaves on backpacks, who participated in fringe sports like cross country and tennis disinterestedly, who skipped class to stand on railroad tracks, throw stones at power lines and smoke cheap cigarettes. At present, looking directly forward, singing R. Kelly's "Trapped in the Closet" along with radio and tapping hand on side of van.

One American-Flag Bandana[3]: What Darren wears, triangle-folded over forehead, stars showing more than stripes.

Hailey naked except for spring-yellow skirt pulled up to waist, on all fours, hair seductively tousled with sweat beading on her hairline, face wincing in that pleasure/pain combination felt only during sex; Darren behind her, cupping a breast in one hand and clasping her waist with the other, groping and

penetrating Hailey on not their guest bed but Alan's bed, the bed he and Hailey sleep in every night, on the sheets they received from Hailey's distant Aunt Catherine at their wedding, knocking against the headboard Alan purchased wholesale from Good Brother's Furniture; this asshole going at his wife, it's *his wife* for Christ's sake, but on they go, even though they know he's watching, maybe even *because* he's watching, Alan a staid, pathetic figure in the corner of the room shrinking fast, down to the size of a stump, a gnome, an insect: Alan's dream on night of 4 July 2017, replaying itself with uncanny clarity upon seeing Darren drive by in van (see similar entries, with slight variations in place, lighting, Alan being/not being physically present, and sexual position for various nights beginning four months previous).

The Present: Series of never-ending moments, played out from one instant to another, in which humanity both perpetually exists and perpetually abandons, evidenced by ambiguous desire to either prolong an un-prolongable moment (see *Sexual Intercourse*) or flee and never return (see current example).

Finally punching out at end of the day: What should be one of Alan's favorite parts of the day but sadly isn't.

Cheap Trucks: 2002 Ford F-150, 2006 Ford Ranger XL, all models Nissan, 2004 Chevy Colorado LS, 1999 Chevy S10, 2000 GMC Sonoma SLS.

Quick dollar-menu dinner, or maybe a stop to check out pricing on new brake pads at Excel: Alan's avoidance-driven contemplations while approaching Van Zeeland Aquamarine Rentals (see *Alan's Dominant Behaviors and Traits*).

Blue Blue Blue: Three colors, of various shades and tones, of Van Zeeland Aquamarine Rentals logo, dolphin jumping over wave encircled in blue floatation device, appearing in no less than seventeen places in Van Zeeland Aquamarine Rentals parking lot, including bar-style light above door flashing with word "Open."

Rockin' Robin: Song originally recorded by Bobby Day, 1958, covered by numerous artists including Paul Anka, U.K. singer Lolly, and Michael Jackson, playing now as jingle of Van Zeeland Aquamarine Rentals door chime, a song Alan loved as a child but, by association, suddenly grows distaste for.

Hailey's Dominant Behaviors and Traits: Humming childhood tunes, consciously or unconsciously; watching and rewatching syndicated 1990s sitcoms; exaggerating; overapplying makeup; recumbent biking and/or treadmill jogging at local Y; hugging; scratching inappropriate places on body at inappropriate times; raising of inflection on last word of sentence to make statements sound like rhetorical questions; eating cottage cheese and/or pickles straight from container after sex; laughing.

Van Zeeland Aquamarine Rentals, Contents: Overhead halogen lighting, bright as a supermarket; one large wood veneer brochure holder, housing pamphlets for various local attractions including Lakes of the Valley tour, Sprangers Apple Orchard, Paperfest

2017, Fox Cities Stadium, Marcus I-Max Cineplex, and Downs Minnow Racing; two moss-green low-back chairs, intended use uncertain; various items for sale, relation to pontoon and Jet Ski rental apparent, including fishing poles, lures, life jackets and can koozies; various items for sale, relation to pontoon and Jet Ski rental less apparent, including pool cleaning nets and wildlife taxidermy; one service counter; one desktop computer connected to cash drawer and credit card scanner; one stool; Darren Van Zeeland.

One American-Flag Bandana[4]: What Darren still wears.

Glance over magazine, forced chuckle, exhalation from nostrils audible even from where Alan is standing, shake of the head, glance back to magazine: Darren's non-verbal response to Alan's entry.

Late[3]: Darren's verbal response to Alan's entry, before Alan even gets a word in edgewise.

Darren: Alan's word, hardly edgewise.

Before you start Chuck: Darren's response to computer screen, example of Darren's aggravating and denigrating habit (see *Darren's Dominant Behaviors and Traits*) of calling all men Chuck and all women Honey.

This Shit: What Alan is not prepared for.

I'll have you know you can't objurgate your way out of a fee just because we know each other: Darren's continuation, still to computer screen.

Dictionary.com Word of the Day, 5 July 2017: Objurgate; previous reference second time word has been misused in Alan's presence, leading him to ponder frequency of use and misuse of Dictionary.com words of the day, leading him to ponder how goddamn ridiculous it is to ponder frequency of use and misuse of Dictionary.com words of the day at that moment.

I wasn't trying to: Rejoinder spoken softly, pathetically half-hearted in nature, by Alan to Darren, a textbook example of Alan's common speech pattern (see *Alan's Dominant Behaviors and Traits*) whereas his ideas mudslide mid-sentence as though someone has interjected or cut him off but in reality has not, leading Alan to wish someone had, what with the painful, resultant pauses in conversation that inevitably follow, though in that regard current example is not textbook (insofar as Alan does not wish to hear Darren speak at all).

Listen Chuck, I'd love to cut you some slack here: Sarcastic response by Darren to Alan (for more sarcastic Darren-to-Alan responses, see entries for 14 March, 5 April, 24 April, 3 May, 7 May, 15 May, 22 May, essentially the entire month of June, 3 July).

But I start making one exception, next thing you know I gotta knock off late fees for every Tom, Dick and Harry that moseys in here. People start thinking, Oh, well, Darren doesn't charge you if it's late anyway, so let's keep it a few more days. No returns, no machines for new rentals. Would that be fair?: Harangue, spouted with exaggerated arm movements, by Darren directly to Alan.

Did you sleep with my wife?: Thing Alan should have said, wanted to say, didn't have the balls to say.

I just hope you don't tackle everything the way you tackle a pothole: Words that flash into Alan's mind, though he can't immediately place their origin until picturing Werny's turkey-shaving-and-mustard-laden mustache.

No, it wouldn't be fair: Alan's first full sentence of 5 July 2017, surprising him, causing him to question how many days previous he's gone this long without really speaking to anyone.

You're right, no it wouldn't. In fact, it'd be pretty damn unfair: Shorter but no less exaggerated remark by Darren, delivered with unnecessarily hostile and animalistic stepping-closer and puffing-up-of-the-chest, enticing in Alan response such threats typically elicit in recipient, a curious concoction of anger and fear.

Darren's Dominant Behaviors and Traits: Smoking Camel Menthol Lights; waterskiing; spending +/- 75% of front desk work time on Facebook, Instagram, or Twitter; ordering brandy old fashioneds despite general distaste for brandy, sugar water, cherries and cloves; gun and bow hunting; playing right-centerfield on multiple beer-league softball teams; playing the victim; referring to all men as Chuck and all women Honey; sleeping in; counting the weeks until his father's business becomes his own; bench pressing and bicep curling; dancing.

I get it, I'll pay. Just chill out: Alan's response, coupled with half-hearted reach-for-the-wallet motion.

Oh Christ, you're gonna guilt me now? Forget it, just forget it: Darren's new overly dramatic and childish I'm-the-victim tactic (see *Darren's Dominant Behaviors and Traits*), leading Alan to consider the fact that if, after five years of marriage, he knows his wife at all, she must be smarter than this.

All right, if you say so: Alan's now emboldened response.

Victory: Achievement of a goal typically, but not always, dependent upon a defeated combatant (see *Loser*) that Alan feels, on levels psychological, financial (25.00 USD), moral and physical (if only slightly).

Ain't a favor for you, Chuck. Consider this one a freebie for Hailey. Tell Honey I said hello: Darren's final power grab.

There: Where that prick had to go.

Yell, "Stay away from my wife, you asshole!"; pull 25.00 USD out of wallet, crumple and throw bills in Darren's direction; storm out: An appropriate response were Alan that sort of person, but he is not, at least not on most days.

Leave quietly, refusing or not refusing to pay; drive truck home where Hailey sits drinking decaf gone cold; silently, without acknowledging her presence, go into bedroom, pack largest suitcase full of any wanted clothes and necessary toiletry items, leaving unnecessary belongings as a biting remark on her

betrayal; exit house; reenter truck and drive off somewhere, anywhere other than here: Alan's desire born four months previous, slightly modified for current situation, growing both further from and closer to actualization multiple times daily.

Pay bill in order to avoid further conflict; never rent from Van Zeeland Aquamarine Rentals again; go home begrudgingly but necessarily; consider opening dialogue with wife about potential affair but instead decide to share reruns of *Friends* and *Frasier* with four cans Pabst Blue Ribbon; sleep: Response most typical of Alan's nature, most likely to be executed on all days preceding 5 July 2017.

The Future: Uncertain.

Roads without Houses

As he slathers the potatoes in coconut oil, Garrett notices the moon's absence for the first time. The window had been installed directly above the inlaid cutting board, and even after years of dinner preparations the moon still surprised him with its stark whiteness, its sun-like brilliance. He had mentioned it to Victoria, remarking on how the light coated the trees like snow. But she was late for an evening spin class, searching frenetically for a missing shoe, and didn't hear.

The gym obsession began two years earlier. Victoria had always been athletic, with a lean, lithe swimmer's body, but she'd read in some women's journal that, after the age of twenty-seven, one loses a pound of muscle and gains a pound of fat each year. Such straightforward, placid arithmetic jarred at her sensibilities as an independent woman, and thus the membership, the six a.m. mixed aerobics and the late-night hot yoga. She flow-charted her escalating workout regimen. She counted caloric intake at every meal. Without alerting Garrett, she excised heavy carbohydrates and excess fats entirely.

In the first few weeks she picked apart Garrett's prepared plates like a child, pushing potatoes and scattering dinner roll bits along the edges. Then she started buying specialized post-workout meals from the gym's café and stopped eating with him altogether.

So in an attempt at solidarity, Garrett joined the gym as well. People do these sorts of things for their marriage, he told himself. But he noticed, from the first time he entered with Victoria, that the gym floor subsumed her entire being, possessed her with a spirit both relentless and singular. She stared only at her face in the wall-to-wall mirrors. She sprinted from elliptical machines to recumbent bikes as though some faceless person would otherwise snatch them up. On the surrounding track she ran as though under medical observation. This carried over to the café, where she pecked bird-like at miniscule salads, and to their drive home, where she raced for changing streetlights and scoffed at other vehicles. It wasn't until she showered and put on pajamas when, at last, her demeanor resembled that of his former wife. But by then it was too late in the night, and there were spin classes in the morning. Sleep always to catch up on. She went to the gym five, six times a week, and so Garrett followed. But more and more, as he watched her mind steel and her body tauten, the entire act—this doing something for their marriage—felt like the exact opposite.

Heat on high, the oil spitting a satisfying hiss, Garrett stares at his potatoes. He hovers a hand over them, feels spackles prick and then burn his palm. He reaches in, pinches one slice that sears his fingertips. He quickly tosses it in his mouth, the heat livening and then just as quickly deadening his cheeks, his tongue, all the way down his throat.

His phone buzzes on the counter, a number he doesn't recognize. With an oil-stained pinkie finger he swipes to dismiss the call, leaving a thin trail like a forlorn country road across the screen. He thinks to call Victoria, to invite her back to dinner, to promise to make something entirely devoid of nonessential fats and simple starches. But he knows she will be rowing leagues along the gym's floor, or climbing a skyscraper's worth of stairs. He knows she won't answer. So instead he grabs the oil bottle with his right hand and drapes the fingers of his left. The oil slides, slickens, runs in the rivers of his palm and under his wedding ring. With a soft nudge the ring slips effortlessly into the sink, where it rolls, like a coin, down into the drain.

Garrett looks to the moonless sky. Then he reaches across the counter to the switch box and flips the disposal, the grating sound of metal trying to destroy metal shrieking through their house.

At quarter past ten Victoria arrives home, her workout clothes hanging over her gaunt frame and her hair in a messy bun. She holds a large bag of gas-station potato chips in her hands. Without a word she goes to the television, turns on a rerun, and consumes the entire bag.

Garrett doesn't speak. He feels, like a massive undertow, the forceful current of her resolve to leave him in everything she's done: the gym, the calorie-counting, the stoic unrest. He watches her seeking an answer that isn't clear, but also isn't him. He sees, like the moonless sky that evening, only a lack.

Letters from the Dead

Marla rereads the letter addressed and written to the deceased Gerald Leland and is just as passionately moved the second time. Gerald may be gone, yes, but he was loved, beloved. She pulls a sheet of overpriced crested paper and her engraved ballpoint she received for her fifteenth anniversary at the post office. *Dear Alice*, she pens, but then crumples the paper and rewrites it in a more robust hand on a new sheet. Any words after the salutation elude her though, as she ponders how to write like a dead man.

She drinks a generous pour of merlot, then another. She tips her head against the wood of her office chair. Her air conditioner revs up, its usual last-ditch attempt before sputtering and then dying. It has been spotty for weeks, and at the height of Milwaukee's humid months. Nearly a year ago her landlord and Marla had come to an unspoken agreement: she wouldn't submit repair requests and he wouldn't have to offer insipid excuses. She tips her oscillating fan directly at her face, the hot air marginally more bearable when in motion.

Hoping it will ignite her romantic side, she brings the glass to her nose, though with age she finds hints of anything, clove or pepper or chocolate or whatever, have long since surpassed her. How will she ever equal Alice's ardor? Her candor? It seems Alice and Gerald haven't seen each other in years. Decades. But even in the honeymoon throes of her marriage Marla hadn't felt such passion for Bruce. They had both grown up in Cedarburg, just north of Milwaukee, in a graduating class small enough to know of one another and yet large enough to never have spoken. She remembered him as slightly overweight, overconfident. It wasn't until, ten years later, an online dating site matched them based on some of Marla's vaguer interests—kayaking, noir films, Brewers tailgates—that she considered him at all. Their dates outdid those she'd had before him, fueled by alcohol and reminisces of a shared, distasteful past. The sex was energetic. They'd married fast; within a year Bruce had spattered their newly shared apartment with framed photos of the wedding, honeymoon, sun-drenched Saturdays at Bradford beach. The photos comforted Marla as Bruce spent more and more time away, their exuberant smiles substituting for physical closeness. But soon enough she realized that the photos weren't about her: Bruce seemed less to love her than to appreciate her for recognizing the obvious fact that he should be loved. For doing what every woman ought to do. When he brashly proposed an open marriage—an idea Marla wasn't patently against, in theory—she saw through the request to the justification for what he must have already been doing. Just two weeks later he fled to the south side with a woman two-thirds Marla's age and looks. Marla's first act was to take all the frames down, but their specter hung in the darkened paint left behind, Bruce's absent face still smiling like an idiot from spotted walls.

In the six months after, Marla has become a bit careless. No, she must admit, reckless. She started scanning the obituaries with the indistinct, morbid hope that she would see Bruce's name. But instead she encountered familial names to match those in the P.O. boxes she filled every day—Branson, Mills, Teggatz. She wondered if the recently deceased Vladimir Swokowski was kin to the Annabelle Swokowski who received weekly student loan consolidation solicitations and subscribed to *Vogue* magazine. Eventually the potent concoction of curiosity and desperation led her to follow those potential connections. And though it wasn't inevitable, when she finally stumbled upon the obituary for Gerald Leland, aged seventy-two, she knew with blind intuition it was the same Gerald Leland who rented box 407.

I am so very elated that you have written me, Marla writes. *It has been so very long.* She stops, considering the countless obstacles one faces when writing letters from the dead. Was Gerald a proper enough man to use full spellings and not contractions, *I am* instead of *I'm, It has* instead of *It's?* Would he use *elated,* or a simpler word like *happy?* As for particulars, she can only be as specific as Alice's letter allows, and no matter how beautifully written it remains frustratingly lacking in detail. Marla consults Gerald's obituary for glimpses, but that too is impersonal, written almost by a stranger: *worked for forty-seven years at Usinger's; loved the outdoors; no wife or children.* She considers following Gerald's paper trail, seeking out acquaintances, gathering snippets and oral histories of his life in order to better respond. She could spend entire weekends trying to find the proper reciprocation. She could spend a lifetime.

But no, she cannot. Mail service to the deceased was rare, often handled and rerouted within the week. For the boxes that weren't detected, junk mail and flyers and magazines accumulated until someone noticed. When Marla had solved that problem in the past by gathering the clutter herself, she bought an extra week, maybe more. Not enough time to foster true correspondence. She has to do this on her own, and now.

Her glass of wine again empty, Marla closes her eyes and tries to see what she has been missing: Gerald and Alice in the brief, budding blossom of their tryst. What had kept them apart? What had prevented them from pursuing the life Alice so fervidly longed for? But the answer, of course, is simple: Alice must have married the wrong man. Her letter an attempt to recapture the past, a life unlived. To reclaim true romance in their twilight, while they still have the chance.

Now that Marla has their story the letter writes itself. She lies on the couch to skim it over, her approval mounting with each new read. Somewhere near the fourth, between Gerald's mellifluous description of his garden and his honest, rueful wish that things had turned out differently, she falls asleep.

Alice's reply arrives days later. Marla drops the letter when she discovers it buried between cable television advertisements. It has the same handwritten address with the swooping G, the same off-white square envelope. She pictures Alice at a candle-lit antique desk, ballpoint pen in dainty but nimble fingers. Or maybe even a white quill with hand-blown ink bottle. A window nearby, drapes flowing in a light afternoon breeze. Her letters come from Crivitz, three hours north, a place Marla has never been. More than anything she needs to read the letter.

Then suddenly, before she can retrieve it from the ground, Marla is blinded by balmy palms. "Guess who?"

Marla winces. She ducks out of Belinda's hands. She bends to the letter and looks back with ersatz nonchalance.

"How's life?" Belinda says. "Hot ain't it?" She fans the rings of sweat under her arms. In her mouth she swirls a pen like a lollipop, gently chewing a cap she will leave anywhere along the office. She has left Cheng alone at the front desk and already a line has formed.

"Yes," Marla agrees. "Even for August."

"Not as hot as my last night, let me tell you."

Without provocation Belinda launches into her night's antics, divulging more detail than their relationship warrants. Marla looks away, this time unwilling to feign interest in the ribald recounts of a woman too old to still believe that happiness is an achievable, lasting state. That life is inherently good. All Marla wants is to be home, in front of a fan, with a glass of wine and Alice's letter. A bead of sweat slides down the middle of her forehead and lands on the envelope. For this she blames Belinda.

Marla turns to her crate, pretending to shuffle through the incoming mail. She ponders various ineffective ways of getting the letter under her blouse with Belinda so close. But then she receives a blessing as Randall, one of their bosses, calls for Belinda from behind the counter.

"Shit, what now?" Belinda says to Marla. "I'll be back. I haven't even gotten to the good part yet. Tootles."

Marla watches her sashay to Randall. She likely bats her eyelashes. Marla has always hated the word *tootles* as a valediction and now understands why. Belinda likely signs emails with *Lates* or *Chow* or *C Ya*, likely *LOLs* and refers to something large as *ginormous*. She works with the written word and, unlike someone like Alice, has no concept of its proper usage. How a simple, elegant formulation of a sentence can take away one's breath. How a carefully chosen word can shoot like a bullet through the soul.

Marla presses the letter to her stomach and slides it down her waistline, untucking her shirt to cover its upper edge. As she continues stuffing boxes, and all the way to the end of her shift, the envelope chafes comfortably against her skin.

Marla reads the letter a dozen times that night, absorbing all the details. *Dearest Gerry,* she begins. So here it is, the shortened name. The familiarity. *Your garden sounds wonderful. Although I will never see it, I feel as though I am there with you now. You always cultivated with such passion. Your plants, your writing. My heart.* Marla smiles at another detail: Gerald was a writer.

I wish I could come to you, Alice continues, *but my heart. It is too weary to handle such travels.* Marla reads on and feels more sorrow than she had in her entire time with Bruce. She wants to reply again but knows she's already on borrowed time. Gerald's box will be cut off soon. This will be the last letter he receives. And if that's the case, it will be a grand exit indeed.

But then her mind delivers the answer, clear and simple. Only three hours away. The return address, *3170 Lake Road,* written in Alice's effeminate hand. Google Earth provides the bird's-eye view of her house's unassuming roof, the triangular lot adjacent to a lake called Noquebay. She needs to go for Gerald, for Alice, for those who have left such vital things unsaid. For anyone on the wrong fork of life's road. She knows it is desperate, insidious even. That she can never mention it to Belinda or anyone. That Bruce, if he knew, would start laughing and possibly never stop. She doesn't care.

The drive to Crivitz takes half an hour more than her navigation's estimate. Off the highway Marla opens her window and watches bushes and farm fields acquiesce to massive, dense trees. Her turns go from straight edges to sloping curves, the labyrinthine roads rising and falling and seeming almost to circle back on themselves. Deep in, her navigation system fails her, some update long since overdue, the satellite recognizing a common road only to surrender to darkness and recalculation. She swears she thrice passes the same straggling buckthorn patch. There's a Lake Drive but also a Lake Circle and a Lake Lane, each road running parallel to Noquebay and then abruptly dead-ending. House numbers too are sporadic, first in the hundreds and finally the thousands, though none near her desired 3170. One of the roads begins each with a W. As she drifts further into the web of northwoods roads she begins to see some intentional, malevolent design, as though the roads exist only to entrap people, to frighten them from ever returning. It is like some mail carrier's nightmare.

So she abandons her car on one of the lake-adjacent streets and walks to the shore. The breeze coming off the lake is thick but pleasant. Here things look more familiar, more like the map she has seen of the place. She is in no hurry; she knows if she traces the shoreline, eventually Alice's lot will reveal itself to her. And anyway, anyone catching her trespassing might prove a useful guide. Like the roads, the shoreline wavers, wooded patches intermittently interrupted with cleared lots and accompanying piers. She removes her shoes and steps beyond a layer of rocks to the sandy brown lake bottom. The water is colder than she expects. A few houses in, a woman bathing in afternoon sun directs her to turn around; a mile later a man mowing around a child-sized play barn confirms she's on the right path.

The sun disappears behind a string of fat, smokestack clouds when she finally sees it. The house looks much the same as the others on the lake, older but maintained, especially in the florid details. Alice has taken care in the shoreline upkeep, with mulch-laden shrubbery islands and a steppingstone walkway and wind chimes that trickle tinny sounds over the waves. In front of large bay windows, six Adirondack chairs in complementary pastels line the house. The air carries the crisp scent of constant movement. Marla pictures Alice's dream here: she and Gerry in the middle chairs, each holding a book of poetry in one hand and gently caressing each other's forearms with the other. Marla takes up one of the chairs, a purplish one, and lets her sweating body slide into the comforting wood. She closes her eyes and allows the tickling chimes, the wind and waves, to all envelop her like an embrace.

And then a click. To her right, atop the large patio, a glass door slides open. Marla opens her eyes but stares ahead at the water.

"Peaceful isn't it?"

Marla turns to the woman who can only be Alice. She is slender, the creases of her skin tight against her wiry neck and arms. Her hair is pure white.

"I'm sorry," Marla stammers as she stands. She waves her hand in a vague direction toward the lake, cursing herself for not even considering an alibi. "I'm actually here with…"

In the silence she flickers her finger as though it will conjure up the flames of a name. But Alice, sweet Alice, gracefully provides the fire.

"The Pluckers? No. The Hahns I wager."

"Yes," Marla says, "The Hahns."

"New friends every week. Herb thinks he owns the lake. Which one you friends with? Violet? Iris? Or Jasmine. You look like a city girl."

"Yes," Marla says. Then, with growing confidence, "Guilty as charged."

Alice descends from the patio. Marla admires her insouciance, her acceptance of this stranger here, in her backyard, using her furniture and her view, but then Marla can't imagine a woman more sympathetic than the Alice from the letters.

"Don't let it fool you though," Alice says, turning back to the lake. "May be only knee-deep most of the way, but it has its traps. A girl once tried to swim across by herself. Nobody makes that mistake anymore."

"You've lived here long?"

"My whole adult life." Alice sighs with the weight of age, with what Marla interprets as regret over the lost opportunity of Gerald. They stand like this for a half-minute, more. Marla wants to continue but is finding Alice more difficult to engage than she anticipated. She expected an immediate invitation into the house, light music, uncorked bottles of red wine. Every part of her just wants to come out and say his name, *Gerald, Gerald,* to open up the history behind the letters, but in haste she has adopted Alice's lie for her, and now must, at least for the moment, navigate the pretense.

"Can I bring you some water?" Alice asks, noting Marla's sweat stains around her neck, under her arms.

"Yes," Marla replies. Then, in a surge of expectation she says, "Actually, would you mind if I use your bathroom?"

Alice hesitates only a moment. "Yes, of course."

Marla basks in the moment she steps inside. It is as she expected, quaint and comfortable, faultless. The table is large, dark, distinctly classic. Alice points her through the kitchen and down the hallway, then retreats to continue the food preparation Marla has interrupted. Marla passes doors to a closet and a study, its shelves disappointingly devoid of literature in lieu of tomes on law. She passes the bathroom. Beyond the entryway, stairs lead to a second level she's tempted to investigate. But then she glimpses the living room and, entering, finds what she needs: a bevy of framed pictures splashed across the eastern wall. They are numerous and of every size. The staggering effect puts Bruce's attempts to shame. In the photos are her children, four sons it seems, from youth soccer to high school graduation to wedding, and then her grandchildren, too numerous and sprawling to count. And then Alice herself, only once photographed alone, somewhere near Marla's age, her hair dishwater blonde and long, her mascara heavy. She wears a look of somber irony. In all other pictures she stands with her unnamed husband, the one she chose over Gerald. Marla has never seen a picture of Gerald, but she has to admit that Alice's husband is handsome, strikingly so, his cheeks slender and his eyes a soft brown. Over the years he has worn beards and mustaches with equal success. He seems one of those lucky men for whom time has only enhanced his allure.

Then she looks across the room, past furniture discordant and yet complimentary, and sees an ornate wooden box atop the mantle. The pieces of the puzzle that is Alice instantaneously topple into place. The box is funereal, containing the remains of this husband, recently passed. It explains perfectly the sudden outreach to Gerald, the wistful melancholia, the poetry. Alice is grieving.

In the bathroom Marla presses a wet hand towel to her forehead. She hears Alice's footsteps in the hallway. When Marla opens the door she finds Alice just on the other side.

"Hope you found the washroom up to par," Alice says.

"You have a beautiful home. I envy you."

"Thank you. Though it's a royal pain to maintain."

Up close Marla notices even more about Alice, the golden bracelet on her wrist with numerous charms, the slight gap between her front teeth, the faint smell of antibacterial soap.

"I have to admit," Marla says, "I snuck a peek at your family photos too. You must be very proud."

"Yes. Yes we are."

Oh, poor soul! The wound of her husband's passing is so fresh that she still slips with the communal pronoun. Marla needs to get to Gerald, needs to pry it out of her, if only for her sake. If Marla reveals herself then, yes, she may need to reveal Gerald's fate too, may need to break Alice's heart all over again. But it will be worth it, if only to hear her verbally recite the poetry of her letters. To usher her back to a lovelier time.

"If you don't mind me asking," Marla says, "what was it like before all that? I mean, before you met your husband. Before your life took such a straightforward path."

"I wouldn't call anything straightforward, dear."

"No, but, I'm recently divorced, and I'm just—I guess I'm having trouble seeing past it."

It's a thin lie, an admission hoping to encourage another, but Alice doesn't take the bait. She instead muses on the commonality of divorce—she was a divorce lawyer, it turns out—and how it is ultimately less of an end than a new beginning.

"Thank you," Marla says. Alice enters one of her blank stares, this time down her hallway. Marla has no more ploys, no other entryways to her needed path. The only thing remaining is the truth. "Actually, I was wondering if we could speak about Gerald."

"Excuse me?"

"Gerald Lel—"

Her voice is interrupted by the loud creak of the front door. Heavy steps enter. Alice turns her attention to them. "Craig, honey," she says. "We're in here."

Footwear shakes to the ground, followed by softer steps down the hallway. A man enters with two plastic hardware bags in hand. Freshly shaved, soft brown eyes, the handsomeness. It is the husband.

"Honey, this is—" Alice shakes her head, looks to Marla. "You know, I don't think we ever exchanged names."

"Kay," Marla says.

"Kay. This is my husband Craig. I'm Penelope. Most call me Penny."

The sound of this woman's real name sends a stifling adrenaline shock through Marla. She coughs, gently at first but then it builds upon itself, billowing in her throat like smoke. Penny rushes to the kitchen for a glass of water. When the cough abates, Marla offers awkward apologies. Craig excuses himself to the work for which he's bought the supplies, some plumbing leak. Marla only wants to leave, and after two more stilted minutes she does, out the patio door. Penny sends her regards to the Hahns. Marla takes up the shoreline, feeling Penny's eyes on her back as she returns helplessly to the lake.

By the time she reaches the road the sky has darkened considerably. She is famished, her body expended. She will find her car but not without struggle. Ahead of her she can see very little, no lampposts marking the streets or car headlights offering temporary glimpses or even moonlight atop the trees, nothing to illuminate her way forward.

Payout

After innumerable hands the machine finally deals Junior three Queens, a winner with a high return, bringing him back up over fifty dollars. Most would feel the rapacious grasp of victory here, but he recognizes the win for what it really is: a ruse, an enticement to lose further. A seditious whiff of hope in an otherwise rigged system. He loses myriad following hands on a single credit bet, biding his time, waiting to catch it. Waiting for the tell. Like a good drinking partner, given enough time every video poker machine will whisper her secrets to you. After forty-odd hands of feeble losing and even feebler winning he finally sees it. There it is, clean as fallen snow. Junior bets his entire credit load and hits deal.

But then something inexplicable happens. He has patiently played it out until now, losing methodically, winning sparsely. He drank three whiskeys and smoked half a pack of Pall Malls. In a hundred bars across Wisconsin he'd done the same, anticipating this moment when the machine revealed herself to him, and was always rewarded with a big winner, a flush or full house or even four of a kind. But instead he sees Jack-high garbage. He holds only the face card, gets even less on the redeal, and loses it all.

He raises his head for the first time in a good while. At the pirate-themed slot machine next to him, an elderly woman has been replaced by a hirsute man with painted fingernails. Five people sit belly-up at the bar, next to each other but clearly not together. The rest of the place is empty. From the bar's speakers an early nineties rock singer begs forgiveness from a past lover.

Junior rises for the bathroom and a sweeping *déjà vu* overcomes him. Like all Wisconsin bars, this place has its peculiarities: miniaturized faux palm trees as tabletop centerpieces, whittled wood taps shaped like fish, a neon blacklit sign garlanded with lacy bras. But also like all Wisconsin bars the overall appearance feels abjectly, scrupulously familiar.

He pisses and then makes for the exit. The tattooed bartender shoots him a skeptical eye as he goes. At his pickup Junior reaches under the passenger seat, his hand prying for and retrieving a fat metal case. A former safe deposit box, the pawn shop cashier had told him, but then Junior never trusted banks, never maintained more than the required minimum in any account. And anyway, how could he explain these furtive earnings? Eighty this night, a few hundred the next: gambling with a consistent wage. He doesn't want to pay the tax and he doesn't want to answer questions. He's spent inestimable hours at the game, has stumbled upon—no, conquered—a complex algorithm that as far as he knows no one else has. To his mind, the money is all his.

He scans the darkened parking lot, peers into the wide windows of the bar. Beyond the glowing name sign with the As burned out—*M rgie Rit 's*—the bartender still watches him. Junior covertly removes the chainless copper key from behind a wedding photo in his wallet. Never has he gone to his earnings like this before: in the past he's always won. In fact he's never opened the box outside of his small space in their apartment's shared garage. But the meddling bartender's concern lies only in Junior skirting his fifteen-dollar bill; he hopes to catch a fleeting license plate if Junior bolts. Junior unlocks the box, planning to pull the first twenty and then close it immediately. But then the tart, clement smell of the cash wafts up to him. He lifts the lid completely. He runs a hand across the top, some newer bills coarse to the touch, almost like sandpaper. Others that have been passed from business to business, from bartender to patron and back again ad nauseam, feel slight and downy, as though they might tear at a gentle touch. Minus this twenty he needs to buy the whiskeys, a nine-month total he keeps on mental tally: currently $82,324.

It is so much, yet takes up little space. Nestled neatly under his passenger seat.

Junior pulls a twenty and reenters Margie Rita's, dropping the bill on the bar without waiting for the bartender to take it. The music, the entire mood has turned melancholic, beckoning him to leave. So he goes back to his pickup and drives off, passing the antiquated downtown of Crivitz and a slew of one-story motels he considers for the night before hitting Highway 41 and trekking the two hours back home.

He arrives well past midnight. Mel is still awake, computer in her lap, a pot of canned pasta and a wooden stirring spoon beside her. On her screen are listings of houses far above their price range. The top one, a colonial on Lake Winnebago, is listed at just below a million. He takes a shower, and returns to find her much the same.

"You should be in bed," he says.

"I'm not the one who has to get up at six."

"Jimmy's birthday. He made us play vodka roulette for an hour. Thankfully I only got two shots."

She doesn't respond to this. Instead she spoons what must be cold pasta rings into her mouth.

"Any luck with the numbers?" he asks. She points to the coffee table, where six halves of lottery tickets lie disheveled atop a magazine. He nods. "Well, someone's gotta win, right."

"Someone's gotta win."

He enters the kitchen area, which is only a few square feet of linoleum with cupboards and undersized appliances. He scrubs a dirtied pot and fills it with water. Waiting for a boil he thinks, as he has more often, about the missed opportunity of those motels: stay the night, then in the morning drive off in any direction away from Kimberly. Start entirely anew. The first time he had the thought, it hectored and shamed him like some high school bully. He tried to ignore it, to be the bigger man. But by then Mel had already begun her slow retreat into herself, appraising her grief in some bracket higher than his own. In truth the stillborn birth of their son—it was a boy, as Junior knew it would be—blindsided him as much as her. He worked hard; he attended Sacred Heart and ingested the young Father Mason's ecstatic sermons without skepticism; he loved his wife with little condition. Aside from the occasional drink and cigarette, he had done little in his life to warrant reprisal. And so the fact that a son would be offered to him and then so needlessly torn away seemed indefensible, egregious. It was utterly unfair. So he decided to mentally arm himself against life's further incongruences by allowing his mind whatever vile, dangerous, inhospitable musings came to it. Seize their power, he reasoned, by indulging them and then letting them go. A catch-and-release of tenebrous thoughts. The problem for him now is that this particular one—the thought of leaving his wife, his hometown, his life forever—won't stop biting his hook.

So he again admits the thought, lets it accumulate on the shores of his consciousness like driftwood. Drive westward to Montana or Colorado, or even south, past Illinois and into Kentucky, Tennessee. Louisiana no more than a day's drive. He of course has enough money, money that Mel doesn't even know he's been saving for one of her lavish houses. Can he be castigated for crashing a wrecking ball through her dream if she didn't know he was building it for her in the first place? It is possible that Wisconsin, for the lifetime of attachments he has made, would not miss him. Same, he could say, for his wife. It is possible that, like a whisper, Junior's former life might just softly resonate into nothingness.

He knows he shouldn't go back. Plenty of bars in plenty of other towns. Ten apiece. He Googles a handful of new places out toward Minnesota, Ladysmith and River Falls, and new bars, The Loose Moose, Tanner's. His circle has necessarily grown, as more bars caught on and word spread. Bar owners, instinctively combative with their cross-town rivals, found a common enemy in Junior. Time came when he needed to dip his toe in the water before diving straight in: he dressed in his usual red-and-black flannel shirt and scuffed Badgers cap and sat at the bar, sipping whiskeys and chatting up whomever sat next to him just to gauge his notoriety. A time when any sort of recognition meant moving on. When changes in ownership shone like unearthed diamonds and his radius was always expanding.

But Margie Rita's nags at him, tickles the back of his throat like a budding cold. Big-city bars, sure, they had newer machines with more intricate algorithms and fail-safes against people like Junior. No matter the con, the game inevitably outmatched the gamester. But he's never lost to an older machine, never failed to master her outdated but still beautifully complex circuitry. His hands, his devout attention, have always yielded results. He has never lost.

◆ ◆ ◆

He returns to a different scene, the bar and tables populated by businessmen in cheap suits and couples and even a family with small children. Junior is unsurprised. It is, after all, a Friday night. He prefers this atmosphere anyway; the anonymity of crowds serves his game well. Though he grew up an only child to a single mother, he always imagined large family life the same: more children, more chance for undetected mischief. More chance to be overlooked.

The same tattooed bartender blends some concoction that he slushes into a plastic coconut shell. Junior approaches to reconnoiter. He wears his only sweater, one with an oversized collar he hates, and has spiked his dark hair with Mel's gel. But his hopes that the bartender will not remember him quickly fall, as without prompting he offers Junior the same brand of whiskey as the night before.

"Tab right?" he says. Up close Junior notices the piercing blue of his eyes, the conscientious lines of his goatee. He smiles at Junior with a disarming familiarity, then nods his head to the back of the bar. "Gonna give it a shot tonight?"

Junior turns to see two men in black shirts setting up tower speakers, lights, a microphone. It is, apparently, karaoke night.

"Not a chance," Junior says. "You want to keep your crowd."

"You'd be surprised at how forgiving they are."

Junior finds an unoccupied high top near the entrance. He feigns interest in a lacrosse match on one of the flat screens, an apparent rivalry between Ivy League schools. He watches the black-donning pair finish their karaoke setup and then acquiesce to a DJ dressed in a Michael Jackson jacket. The flamboyant DJ clears his throat, checks for sound, and wastes no time entreating the bar patrons to step forward. But it's too early—the sun not yet down, the liquor not deep enough in their blood—and so after fruitless prodding he threatens to sing himself all night if no one else will. His screeching rendition of "Billy Jean" validates the threat.

Junior lights a cigarette and settles into his stool. He keeps a distant eye all the while on the bartender, on a female server who has taken up her shift and circulates the tables. A young man, his age or less, occupies the pirate slot machine but the poker machine sits unattended, seductive, waiting. One more whiskey. It never hurts to be oversure, a lesson he learned early in his tenure at a bar called Shotsky's. The waitress was handsy and flirtatious; he'd subsequently had too many tequilas. Near bar close he finally cashed out with over $7,000. The bartender studied him like a skittish pit boss. The whole bar turned its attention as Junior doubled-down on his act, playing the part with zeal, shouting about a made-up divorce and backlogged child support, proclaiming he'd never won so much as a three-dollar scratch-and-win, demanding his beginner's luck. Instead of his money he got dragged out of the back door and thrown unceremoniously into a dumpster. When he hit the trash his shoulder dislodged, shooting a searing pain into his whole body. He tried to stand, but in his drunken state he found footing on the slippery refuse elusive. Ultimately he passed out. A few hours later he came to, rising with the sun, the night's bags of empty bottles and half-eaten scraps atop him. He had a pounding in his head and urine soaked through his pants. The worst of the whole ordeal was the next half hour as, stuck there in the dumpster, he fought through white-blinding pain to jerk his shoulder back into place.

After that incident he attempted more sedated venues: airports, coffee shops, supper clubs. He was surprised by how many places housed video poker machines when he decided to look. But the bright lights, the sober and alert patrons and workers, the relative composure, all played against him. There was no place he knew where anonymity and showmanship mixed together so well as a small-town Wisconsin bar.

So he waits, and just when his window seems to open—as the mother of the family graciously relieves the DJ with a Disney number for her children—the door slams open beside him and a woman enters. She is an attention seeker and knows it. She wears a tank top under her jacket, a leather skirt above the knee. She saunters straight to the bar and orders a shot and a beer. She shares a laugh with the bartender, a quick but gentle touch on the wrist. One of the cheap businessmen immediately approaches and orders a drink beside her, his buddies conspicuously watching how it will play out. She catches Junior in a stare for a moment too long. He looks away and approaches the machine, imagining her eyes on him the whole while.

At the machine he shakes the woman from his mind, tunneling his vision on the more profitable gamble. He has determined to take it slow this time, to woo the machine, to give her the romance she needs in order to reveal her true, deeper secret. He won't let her fool him again. He starts as always with forty dollars in credits and bets the minimum regardless. He loses, loses, hits a high pair and gets some back. He plays for half an hour as the sun sets and the family leaves. Another of the businessmen tackles a bland rendition of Journey as the machine flashes before Junior: there it is again. The tell. Naked in front of him. He intuits the next hand to be a straight, paying back four to one. A net of $64.50 if he bets it all. But he doesn't. Instead he keeps with the minimum, and as the cards fall into place—a four, a five, a six, an eight, and the Queen he will scrap—he feels the unmistakable presence of the waitress over his shoulder.

He turns to her. She is petite, blonde. He imagines her shopping in the juniors section at particular stores. Under the businessman's middling Steve Perry she asks to refresh his whiskey, even though his first is half full. The bartender observes them from afar.

This is the part of his game he likes least: the constant charade. He not only has to caress the machine; to do it right he also has to navigate the bartender or owner who pays him, the waitress who serves him drinks, and any number of onlookers who might catch wind of his escalating credit and hover near, hoping to gravitate in his auspicious aura. Basically, for a decent-sized payout, Junior has to play the part for the entire bar.

"Of course," he says. The waitress smiles. She turns and so does Junior, but before he can even reorient himself to the game he hears, "Make that two, doll."

It is the woman. Up close her features become more definite, her eyes a bit too spaced, her lips rouge and full. Her hair contains streaks of a dark purple dye. Junior wants to hit his straight but he accepts her intrusion instead.

"It's like this," she says to him. "You may be the most intriguing guy in this bar right now, but it's not a position you're used to."

Junior laughs. "And you can tell that how?"

"The sagging shoulders. The darting eyes. You look ridiculous in that sweater by the way."

"And your skirt is too tight."

"Ahh!" she says, slapping Junior with some force on the shoulder. She steps closer, the smell of her overapplied lilac perfume carrying to him. "Feisty too. Good. I'm Sheyla."

"That's a fake name."

She scoffs, then digs into a tiny purse hanging from a spaghetti strap to retrieve her driver's license. Sheyla Johnson, born 1989. Address in Wausaukee, the next town over.

"So fuck you."

"Fair enough. I'm Junior."

"Sounds just as fake."

The waitress returns with identical whiskeys. Junior places his beside his other one; Sheyla tips her head back and jettisons hers with one gulp. She flickers her license between two fingers before returning it. "It's been Wisconsin my whole damn life. Come tomorrow though it'll be California."

"Tomorrow, huh."

"I'm destined. But don't get any ideas. I'm not taking on hitchhikers. This is my adventure."

"Wouldn't dream of it. Though I don't think you'll make it in a day."

The bar has quieted, the karaoke losing any small luster it may have had. The DJ fills the void with Prince's "Little Red Corvette," his voice playing better in softer tones.

"Well, nice knowing you, Junior. If that's really your name. Check for me in the movies." She looks at the machine for the first time. "Ditch the queen and you're aces."

He thanks her for the advice. At the bar, she resumes her flirtation with the bartender. And so he again puts her from his mind and holds the low cards. He hits redeal. With a single flip the game undresses in front of him, rewarding him with the gut-shot seven of hearts he was expecting all along.

The karaoke fizzles completely an hour later, replaced by a jukebox that a group of younger women plugs with nonstop country. The businessmen too have been replaced by a pack of either underage or just-age guys, all wearing backward hats and drinking straight from pitchers with ardent attention. The bartender has turned his focus to them, waiting for the inevitable spill. Sheyla remains at the bar. Like a child she circles the straw in her glass, but then takes down half with each draw. Junior has slowly worked his way to a respectable credit near $120: the machine, though predictable now, is slower than most, less willing to dangle her high-return hands for a real payday. He smokes more than usual, the air above him lingering like fog. When the waitress returns he orders another whiskey. When Mel buzzes his cellphone he ignores it. After another few minutes he spies Sheyla on her way over, flagging down the waitress in the process. She orders something Junior knows he will pay for. She pulls a stool from the vacated slot machine and sets it down, close.

"Okay, you win. You are the most interesting guy here. Congratu-fucking-lations."

"I don't think you're giving my competition proper credit. That guy in the Marines shirt nearly hit the 'Take On Me' high note."

"You don't want to know why I find you interesting?"

"I thought it was my sweater."

"Don't get cute." The waitress delivers two more drinks. Sheyla hands him one. "You've been at this machine for over an hour and haven't plugged extra money. So you're lucky. And luck, my friend, is an animal that travels in packs."

"You may be right about that." He rings his credit up more than he should. "Care to test your theory?"

Without hesitation Shelya reaches across his body and hits deal. The hand is a sucker's bet, three unconnected face cards that will yield nothing on the redeal. They lose swiftly.

"Guess you were wrong."

"One hand does not luck make," she replies. "Let's see how this plays out."

And so they play, though Junior knows the flavorless monotony of such games left to their own. Some nights the more mulish ones have trouble keeping even Junior's attention. So as he flitters away five dollars in petty bets he watches Sheyla's eyes drift from the machine and back to the bartender, who has taken interest in their budding bonhomie. She tinkers with a fray near her chest. Any more of this and Junior will lose her. He offers to let her play a few hands; she declines. He tries small talk, asking questions about her pending cross-country trip, and after another drink—and another moderate win—she loosens a bit. She likes waterskiing; her father lives on a local lake. Surfing will come easily. She plays the lottery too, the biggest ones. "Why win small? These machines," she says, prodding the wood panel like an older sibling, "are for chumps."

"Not necessarily true."

"Yes, necessarily true. Slow bleeds still kill you, and are more painful to boot. The only way to win is to go for broke and hit the motherload."

"You're wrong. You can be good at poker the same way you're good at, say, engineering. It's all math."

"So why aren't you an engineer then?"

"My mom tried. Just because you're good at something doesn't mean it's interesting."

"Amen, brother."

She excuses herself to the bathroom. Junior plows through a number of losing hands in her absence, racing toward the big win that will keep her beside him. But that is the problem with Sheyla's mentality, indeed the mentality of most gamblers: their lottery-winner optimism. The day Junior abandoned that was the day the machines began to disrobe before his eyes. The credit amount doesn't matter to the machine; it's the amount of hands won or lost. Fish long enough without a catch and she'll send a nibble. Junior simply needs to recognize when that fish is coming; more importantly, he needs to know when it will be a miniscule panfish or a contest-winning largemouth bass. And just a moment after Sheyla returns, there it is, the massive tug on his line: a whopper, a big-gamer. A tournament winner. Junior smiles at Sheyla. "I've got a feeling here."

"Are you nuts? All you've done since I showed up is lose and more lose." She raps the screen with a fingernail. "What's the opposite of *let it ride?*"

"It's called *trust your gut,*" he says. He racks up his credit load theatrically, to half, then three quarters, her surprise mounting. She holds her breath. He reaches his total, just shy of $225. His finger hovers over the deal button. Then she smiles back and slams her hand over his, the pulse in her thumb thundering into his wrist.

"Balls to the walls," she says.

Junior expects a lot of face, or a common suit, but the machine throws him another curveball: a pair of sixes with ace-high. No straight draw, only a puncher's chance at the spades. She has served him last night's subterfuge yet again, teasing with goods she hasn't delivered, offering a promise she hasn't kept. Sheyla's lips curl in concern but then she sees Junior watching her. She kicks back and laughs, unwilling to divulge her genuine investment.

"You're royally fucked," she says. "Better hold that ace and pray for another."

He glowers at the cards. The ace is a dupe, the red herring. He holds the sixes and the next highest card, a queen. "That is beyond stupid," she says, but he hardly hears her. This is it, he knows. The money and the girl's attentions, all or nothing. He bites his lip and hits redeal, hoping for the blind luck to hit the full house the machine benevolently delivers.

Shelya screams with delight. The whole bar turns to them. Her hands fly around his neck. The credits roll up and up, past double, triple, quadruple his money. They land near $1500. She cranes Junior's head and kisses him. Her elation surges from her lips, from her fingers grasping at the base of his neck.

"See," he says when she pulls away. "No luck necessary."

"Wow. That was amazing. How'd you know to hold the—
" She curls flung strands of hair behind her ears. "You know what, fuck it. I don't even want to know. This calls for shots."

She orders spiced rum that sticks in Junior's throat. When she calls for another she shares a pointed look with the bartender, and all at once the duplicitous possibilities enter Junior's mind: Sheyla is a hoodwinking player herself, getting a free night's drinks or more from winning gamblers like him. California a ploy, perhaps even her license too. He indulges the thoughts even further: she's in cahoots with the bar, a hired hand summoned to expose his scam. Junior's reckoning not just for Margie Rita's but for all the bars across Wisconsin. His arrears come to roost in the form of a beautiful vixen. Just like Shotsky's, Junior's credit ticket will earn him only his comeuppance, though this time much worse than a separated shoulder and a dumpster. Junior's own devil, this Sheyla, deliverer of his divine retribution.

But if he's willing to go that far—a long shot by any standard—then he must travel the opposite way as well. He has always played alone, kept his cards close to the chest, withheld his trick from everyone. But even magicians have assistants. He imagines the two of them roaming westward together, a different bar every night. A hundred fabricated meetings and enacted victories. In his head surges their second rum and a distinct *presque vu*, a feeling that this night will prove crucial, and yet what it is, what its importance will be, eludes him. He is falling, but cannot decipher where on this sliding scale from doom to paradise he will land. But he also doesn't care, the liquor flowing a peaceful warmth down his entire body. He turns his mind from the future, from thoughts of Sheyla beneficent or nefarious, and continues to do what he does best: play.

♦   ♦   ♦

He wakes, alone, in a begrimed motel room. The bedside clock reads 4:12. A dim reading lamp shines in his face. A heater in the corner hums unevenly like a car failing to start. He rubs at his piercing headache as the drive to the motel, the remainder of the night, plays back to him in discordant shards. He knows from drunken nights past that if he doesn't recall these flashes now they will, like a dream, evaporate into his unconscious. That the trail will abruptly go cold. He sees himself with Sheyla on this bed, kissing and groping over their clothes, his besotted yearnings warring against a desire to be faithful. Then the bar, cashing out with unnecessary flair and antagonism. He digs into his pocket, past his phone abundant with missed calls, for the credit receipt. It reads 9,248. Just about $2,300.

A car passes and its headlights briefly shutter into the room. Junior sits up with a grunt, the crown of his forehead dizzying in pain, and pats his pants pockets. His wallet is gone. He rises and checks the bathroom, inside every drawer, knowing of course that the money is gone too.

Then his mind recovers the drive. Junior too drunk but of course he wouldn't leave his pickup. Sheyla's voice, egging him to cruise about town, nostalgic for places she would soon willfully abandon. It was raining; he recalls refracted streetlights on his windshield, a pleasant drumming against his roof. They drove and drove, for how long Junior didn't know, Sheyla sitting all the while in his passenger seat.

He rushes out of the motel to the narrow parking lot. The rain sings in puddles dappled about the pavement. His truck is parked across two stalls. He pauses at the passenger door, takes a breath that sharpens his blurred vision. Then he throws open the door, expecting his box too to be gone but there it is, nested as always, its dull chrome hidden within the black cloth of the cab carpet. It is still there.

His adrenaline gives way to a thick and unsettled lethargy. He picks up the box. Underneath his larger relief foments a timorous, foreboding sense of fragility. That he almost lost it all. That everything could hang on such tenuous moments as this.

He arrives home at half past six. He stomps the morning rain from his shoes. On the foyer, next to his work boots, rests a packed duffel bag and a pillowcase filled with clothes. Mel is not in the living room or the kitchen but the bedroom, asleep facedown on the bed, fully dressed in jeans and coat and shoes. She looks oddly at peace.

She has something she needs to say. If he had answered any of her calls, she might already be gone. Junior goes to their small kitchen table and pulls a chair and awaits what is coming to him. He will bear in silence Mel's words and then, after she has let him have it, he will let her decide for herself whether or not to hold him. She will decide, finally, if Junior has indeed been a losing hand from the start.

Kindred's Mother

Kindred's mother was nineteen when she gave birth to a five-pound, fifteen-ounce girl with no hair and one arm slightly longer than the other. Kindred's father stood by her side, his arm bearing transferences of her pain, his reassuring whispers drowned in the cacophony of childbirth. After thirteen hours Kindred arrived with no complication. Nurses wiped her face and distended head, swaddled her in breathable blankets, weighed her. Kindred's mother declined to hold her. She abandoned the hospital and her daughter's life the next day.

With the child left unnamed, her father stood behind the plate glass window watching the room outlined with blue and pink bassinets. Some babies slept; some lay mouths agape, their unsettling eyes attempting to figure out this new world into which they'd been ceremoniously thrust. A few wailed and would not be consoled. A passing nurse pointed out his girl to him. He left the hospital that night after standing for three hours, watching his fallow child sleep through whimpers and cries, calm amidst the chaos. She needed a name; at least he could give her that. He decided on Kindred, Kindred Baxter:

the first name his gift, the last her mother's. Once given the seedling of a name, her future blossomed before him. Jungle gyms turned to tumbling tracks turned to high beams. An ace at spelling and math, highest grades in her class. She developed her own brand of woman through angst and joy, through great failure and even greater success. Prom with a handsome and affectionate boy, esoteric literature in her free time, cheap horror movies with friends on Friday nights. Everyone called her Kindy, or just Kay; everyone except her father, who always addressed her by her full name. That night, he drove through hard rain that turned into a cold, ceaseless sleet, across four state borders and never returned.

Kindred's mother returned to her empty apartment. A renovated attic of an elderly couple's home, it had one bedroom and a kitchen/living area divided by an obtrusive knee wall. She had no television, no phone. She preferred night shifts; on her off nights she lay restless in her frameless bed, in her miniscule bedroom, dreaming of the life she'd envisioned before all this. The life that once seemed effortless. She found regret, like love, would not be deterred. Despite herself she dreamed of life's reclamations, where orphan children reunite with their birth mothers. Like protagonists in some grandiose redemptive novel, they narrate every detail of their lives, pausing often to express how wonderful it is to finally meet. For the thousand speculative images and scenarios in their minds to finally crystalize. Their relationship commences with a freshness that neither has ever known, their bond all the stronger for their trials.

Kindred's ruminations, however, tended to manifest themselves outwardly. At eight, in a foster home in East St. Paul, Kindred woke earlier than the other two children and took to their faces with magic markers. With the lightest touch she sketched a playground with a merry-go-round and swings on Timmy's left cheek, and then a vivid sunset sloping down the horizon of Jessica's nose. Everyone knew Kindred as the culprit, but that didn't stop the other children from warming to her, from following her improvised rules for candlelight tag and ghost in the graveyard, from playing a part in Kindred's numerous directed plays. When she led them in an abbreviated version of *Hamlet*, Timmy and Jessica and even Kindred—playing both Hamlet and Ophelia—recited with gusto words they didn't understand.

The Gardners from Apple Valley were Kindred's first family to speak of adoption. She was ten. They had another adoptee, a lanky fourteen-year-old named Natalie, who by then was seasoned as the elder statesman. As she developed into a teenager herself, Kindred settled into a mutual understanding with the Gardners about their roles. Mark and Janet were orderly, affectionate in a formal way; Kindred regarded them more as teachers, as authority figures who deserved respect but not quite love. She declined to call them Mom and Dad. Often, during family dinners or board game nights, Kindred stared idly out the window, chin rested in her palm and eyes far away. She wanted to give them more—nightly cheek kisses and teenage secrets and her undivided attention during Game of Life spins and Monopoly dice rolls—but she found that she couldn't force affection any more than she could force the setting sun to suspend, reverse course, and return to its zenith in the sky. She didn't even want to change her former life, it wasn't that; however, staring out that window, her desultory thoughts inevitably led her to alternative futures.

When they dropped Natalie off at college in Milwaukee, as the family bode an ebullient farewell, Kindred cried for twenty minutes in her arms. No one knew what to do. Janet petted her hair; Mark tried a hand on her shoulder. Natalie whispered that this wasn't the end, that the family would visit, that she'd return any possible weekend. Still Kindred didn't let go. In truth she was as surprised by this outburst as they were, her tears and tremors spontaneous and involuntary. She was embarking on new territory as well, high school, and as all three of her family members attempted to comfort the wrong person, Kindred herself justified it as simply adjustment overload. The loss of the closest thing she'd had to a real sibling. But when she finally freed Natalie into her new dorm, into her new life, she recognized it as more than that. On their drive back to Minnesota, as they passed used car lots and obtuse billboards and cow pastures and metal irrigation sprayers and even a llama farm, Kindred knew her tears included a hint of envy, of the fact that she would have to wait four more years before finally being able to decide her own path.

Kindred returns home from school a year and a half later, slinging her book satchel in a corner along with her shoes and spring jacket. She goes straight for the pantry. In a short while Janet will take her Driver's Ed at the midtown Sears. Only two more in-class sessions before behind-the-wheel and then, she figures, easy sailing to all the limited but consequential freedoms of a license.

Janet arrives an hour later to find Kindred on the couch with her head in the pages of *Richard III*. Their ten-year-old orange tabby reposes happily on her chest. Her hair drapes over the armrest and sprawls down the couch like some exotic plant. She licks a finger to turn the page. "You're late," she says, never looking up from her book. "Third time this week."

"Tax season." Removing her suit jacket, Janet enters the kitchen and immediately pulls plastic containers of leftovers from the refrigerator. "Did you eat? Is your father home yet?"

"Nope and nope." Kindred dog-ears her page and goes to the kitchen island. She rolls a placemat into a tube and peers through one end to the kitchen window, where their tabby leaps atop the sill. *"Out of my sight!"* Kindred recites. *"Though dost infect mine eyes."*

"Aspen, off," Janet says. "I'm sorry Kindred, what was that?"

"Nothing." Kindred keeps up the gaze, enjoying the singular, pigeon-hole perspective of Janet's mint plant beside their disobedient cat, the salt shaker, the white dishwasher. Of seeing the world only one piece at a time. She turns to the door just as it opens. "Speak of the devil."

Mark enters with an exaggerated flourish, his tie unevenly loosed on his neck and a glaze of sweat on his forehead. He carries a briefcase in each hand. "What are you still doing here?" he asks Kindred. His hair is littered in all directions. He drops the cases to run a hand through it, but within seconds it scatters to its original jumble.

"Nice to see you too," Kindred says.

"It's my fault," Janet says.

"You tell that to Lippart," Kindred says. She sets the placemat down and it unfolds itself perfectly into place. "Last time he paused a grotesque car crash video just to lecture me on the virtues of punctuality."

"Lippart. I swear," Mark says, moving to sit but then thinking better of it. "Did you eat? Let's move."

"Working on it," Janet says. The timer on the microwave and the doorbell ring one after the other. All three look to the door.

"Impeccable timing," Kindred says, bounding from her stool.

"If it's those religious zealots," Mark calls, "tell them the Lord wants my daughter to pass Driver's Ed."

Walking down the hall, she slides a hand along the floral wallpaper trim on either side, as though spreading wings to fly. She brings her hands together with a clap. She peeks through the triangle windows on the door but doesn't recognize the woman on their porch. She opens the door. And then, instantly, before the woman can even look up, she knows.

Her face is youthful, though when Kindred looks closer she sees signs of premature age: stray facial hairs covered in makeup, crow's feet at her eyes. Gray hairs sprouting at her roots. But there Kindred is also, in the small ring of blue within her hazel eyes. And in the tilted crease of her smile. She wears a pastel blue dress, heavy eyeliner, and an unmistakable look of expectation.

"Kindred?" Mark calls from the kitchen. Kindred's mother tilts her head at the sound of Kindred's name. "We gotta get going sweetie." Then Mark's hand on Kindred's shoulder, the door opening fully behind her. In a flash he is outside, pushing past Kindred with more force than he intends. He lets the door slam behind him. Kindred retreats, hearing only Mark's imperceptible voice in a raised whisper.

Janet appears near the stairway moments later with a leftover burrito on a paper plate. "Who was that?"

But Kindred has no reply. She watches the door, knowing it will reopen at any moment but not knowing what she will see. Janet peers out the triangles. Her sunken expression confirms Kindred's suspicion that this is not her mother's first contact.

When Mark returns, he and Janet exchange a look pregnant with concern. But then Mark turns to Kindred, adopting his previous urgency. "We've got to get you to class, honey."

In the car, Mark blasts his classic rock station. The armrest rattles under Kindred's hand. They pull into the mall complex before Kindred finally reaches over and shuts it off.

"We going to pretend that didn't just happen?"

Mark idles in front of the building. A group of disenfranchised teens exits the adjoining supermarket with bagsful of boxed candy. Kindred recognizes one of them; they share an awkward wave.

"You should get inside," Mark says.

"How long has she been looking for me? At least you can tell me that."

Mark worries the cuticle of one thumbnail with the other. "A few weeks. I—we just thought that, well. We want what's best for you. And there's legal issues, ones that we want to make sure—"

"Tell her I'll meet her," Kindred interrupts. Mark looks at Kindred for the first time. She opens her door. "Call Natty first. I would like her there with me."

She closes her door. Mark calls something unintelligible behind her. She arrives during one of Lippart's lectures, this on the right of way, but doesn't receive the reproach she expects. He seems resigned to her indifference. And so when her attention falters, when he calls on her but finds her staring blankly out the classroom window, he simply moves on.

◆ ◆ ◆

The tires of Mark's sedan screech a high-pitched wail as Natalie jerks to a halt. She has always driven recklessly, with flitting attention, even on the tangle of one-ways and numbered streets near downtown. She searches in vain for a parking spot right outside their destination. "Jesus H," Natalie says as she loops around. "You want me to just drop you off and meet you in front?"

The sky is painted in wispy brushstroked clouds. Kindred declines. They rove blocks filled with incompatible buildings, historically revived restaurants abutting new highrise apartment complexes. They have agreed to meet Kindred's mother at Espresso Royale, a college coffee shop in the heart of Dinkytown, a place Kindred frequents with friends whenever they get the trendy urge to ride the light rail and feign independence. The Royale is eclectic, sprightly. Waits for tables are frequent. No two chairs or tables match. Cultural music competes with the consistent ching of the vintage cash register and rhythmic hum of the frother. Most patrons read alone from thick college textbooks, or speak in small groups at huddled couches. Whenever she goes, Kindred tends to ignore her friends, choosing instead to bask in the tumultuous solitude. It is a place where she feels both surrounded and peaceably alone.

They finally find a spot; Kindred feeds the meter with the money Mark gave her. Natalie leads down the busy sidewalk, fitting right in with her skinny jeans and ragtag haircut. She has adapted to college life as fluidly as everyone knew she would. She struts with confidence but stops every few steps to check back on Kindred, as though each time Kindred will have fled.

They turn a corner past a used bookshop and the Royale appears. Kindred stops. Her mother is in the window, at a small nook with three unoccupied cushioned chairs surrounding her own. A group of students looking for seats breaks her wistful gaze; she excuses them away. Kindred instinctively slides behind Natalie, as though her mother will at any moment catch sight of her. As though that would matter.

Throughout Kindred's adolescence, her fellow foster children always invented romanticized lives for their birth parents. One boy, whose name she can't remember, placed every job he desired upon his father: first astronaut, then fighter pilot, then curer of virulent diseases. A younger girl named Jane Retton believed her mother to be the famous Olympic athlete Mary Lou. Leonard dutifully watched *Masters of the Universe* and imagined his father as He-Man, ready one day to swoop into the house with sword and oversized shield, rescue Leonard, and abscond to everlasting happiness. Unlike them, Kindred accumulated and pocketed her imagined lives, locking them away in the treasure chest of her heart. They belonged to her and no one else. So the sight of her mother now, in the window of her coffee shop, gives her pause. She wonders if it would have been easier to be the others, if a disproportionate lie might actually soften the blow of the truth.

Natalie notices Kindred's reticence. She places a hand on her shoulder. "You know, I can go in there and tell her the bet's off. If you don't want—"

"I want to. I do."

"All right. But maybe you should lead." Natalie steps aside. "In fact, maybe we should have, like, a safety word. In case you want to bail." She looks around them, searching for the proper inspiration. "How about, I don't know, *cappuccino.*"

"We're going to a coffee shop."

"*Flightless birds* then."

"There's no plausible way to work that into a conversation."

"Okay, Shakespeare. You come up with something better."

Kindred passes, keeping her eyes forward. She walks half a block out of the way to avoid the window. The door to the Royale jangles its Christmas-style bells. Kindred joins the line snaking around the condiment island, feeling all the time her mother's eyes on her. She orders a specialty latte, Natalie a tall black coffee. As the baristas prepare their drinks, Kindred knows she can keep this up only so long. She glances over and sees her mother, staring straight at her.

She wears a ruffled, summery blouse that drapes over a dark skirt. Less makeup this time, her face exuding a natural beauty in the window's streaming sun, a feminine handsomeness. She rises when they approach. She extends her arm, saying, "You must be Natalie. A pleasure." Natalie accepts the greeting and occupies the corner seat. "And Kindred, I've—thank you for coming. I feel like I've been waiting my whole life."

"That's heavy," Natalie says after letting out a thin whistle. Kindred shoots her a look but is grateful not to have to respond. She accepts her mother's outstretched hand. It seems as though her mother would hold on forever, so Kindred breaks the handshake by sitting.

"I wasn't sure you would—" her mother says. She perches on the front half of her seat, hands on her knees. To Kindred, the setup feels like a staged-for-TV interrogation, though she can't determine appropriate roles. "You can't know the relief."

"I can imagine," Kindred says. Her mother startles at her voice. Kindred wonders if every small revelation about her will bring the same stupefaction.

In the corner opposite them, a guitar-wielding man strums three cords in succession. Few people seem to notice. At a nearby table, two women puzzle through an organic chemistry equation. Somewhere behind her, a man with a deep voice offers an insincere apology.

"Well, now we're here," her mother says. "I'd like to know about you. Everything you care to tell me. School, social life. Boyfriends. Everything there is to know about my daughter."

"No," Kindred says, more sternly than intended. "You first."

"Oh, okay. Let me see. Where to start? I was raised in. . . Wait, you probably don't care about that, right? I'm the senior manager at—"

"That's not what I meant," Kindred interrupts. "I want you to tell me about me. Where I came from. Why I was born."

Natalie nods at Kindred. Her mother presses each finger of her hands together in a unified pattern, from thumb to pinkie and back again. The uneasy habit is one Kindred finds herself performing often. Then her mother begins.

Kindred's father was high school royalty, letterman in football and basketball, purveyor of good times. A freshman when he was a senior, Kindred's mother became perilously tongue-tied when passing him in the hall between classes, and only in her private midday fantasies could she hold his hand, kiss his cheek, wear his jacket. But then three years passed, and she became the senior. On homecoming weekend every one of her friends hosted a party and she, ever gregarious, attended each. At one of them—Stacy's or maybe Rick's, she couldn't remember—she saw him again. Who approached whom she also didn't recall. But his added years, the extra bulk and short mustache, further enchanted her. He was still a king.

Kindred's conception occurred two months and a few dates later. On her eighteenth birthday, she told her parents; the next day they expelled her from their house. Kindred was born at St. Elizabeth's Hospital at 9:37 in the morning. Two days later she was motherless and fatherless and bestowed only a name.

Natalie watches Kindred through the entire story. As her mother awaits Kindred's response, Kindred turns to her sister. "Think we could have a minute?"

"You sure?"

"You won't go far."

Natalie rises, takes her mug to a table just a few feet away that a ponytailed guy shares without hesitation. Kindred's mother leans forward, willing the physical gap away. Kindred imagines her holding out her hand.

"It's one thing," Kindred says, "to know you were a mistake. It's another to hear it in story form."

"No no no," Kindred's mother says. "I was. . . we were young, and I didn't love your father. I was afraid and alone. I was in no position to—" She runs her fingers along her eyelids and traces them like tears down her cheeks. "I never said you were a mistake."

Natalie gives a throat-clearing cough. At the counter a barista-in-training fails to contain a foam overflow. "*If you can look into the seeds of time,*" Kindred recites, "*and say which grain will grow and which will not, speak then unto me.*"

"I'm sorry?"

"Nothing."

Her mother bites a tiny section of her lower lip. "Kindred, I'm in a better place now. I just got a promotion. I rent a house. It's in Wisconsin, on the east side of the state, but it's nice. There's a lake just outside of town." She performs her finger tick again, this time more hurriedly. "I don't want you to move, or anything. They're your parents now. I get that. I guess what I'm asking for is, I don't know, a chance. To do at least some of the things I haven't. To be what I should have been."

Unsurprised by this confession, Kindred still finds herself without a reply. What else did she expect? Kindred focuses her gaze again, this time on a small, dark freckle under her mother's right eye. Kindred envisions black and purple marker streaks across her mother's face, tracing themselves beneath her cheekbones, along her jawline. But the whole picture refuses to form; she can't see beyond fragments, beyond disconnected lines.

"You've given me my name," Kindred says. "I'm very sorry, but right now that's all I want from you. Someday I might feel differently. If that's the case, I'll come to you."

Her mother gasps. Her jaw hangs slack. Kindred rises. The coffee shop around them buzzes, blissfully unaware. Many apropos Shakespeare quotes rush to Kindred's mind, ones about loss and regret and love. Kindred would reach out a consoling hand, if it wouldn't only complicate things further. Instead she offers a heartfelt goodbye, her last words now and possibly forever, and exits the coffee shop.

Natalie waits until the Royale is out of sight before stopping Kindred. "What the hell happened?"

"Nothing I wasn't expecting."

"Well Christ. That went from zero to sixty in a hurry. You could have given me some warning."

"Flightless birds."

Natalie throws a playful jab at her shoulder. "That guy was cute. I could've gotten his number."

"And start a long distance relationship?"

"Ha. Like there's any other kind."

Natalie's words hang in Kindred's mind as they reenter Mark's car. She knows she will love someone, profoundly and without restraint, some day. It may be a man or woman she hasn't yet met; it may be Natalie, the Gardners. Her mother. It may even be her own child. She knows this love will be undivided, unfettered by all that life has chosen for her before it. She knows it will be her own.

To Play Hockey, One-on-One

Barry knows he will pay for this in the morning. He misses a loop on his brown single-blade skates and must retract the laces entirely to start over. Once corrected he stands; his right wobbles a little, but his left feels altogether too tight. But is it too tight? Skates have to be snug so you don't twist an ankle, like he's damn sure he will if he doesn't give his right laces at least another tug. Either way his feet will puff and swell into miniature clubs at the end of his legs. He takes a pull from his bottle of brandy. What exactly the hell is he thinking? He hasn't played hockey in twenty-two years.

It is New Year's Eve. The lake froze over two weeks previous, prompting all local ice fishermen to chance their pickups onto the center, wooden shanties dragging in tow. The sun wanes, and though the day isn't particularly cold, by night it will plunge below zero in a hurry. Many trucks have fled, their drivers likely frequenting one of the four bars on the lake. A select few weather the night in their shanties with battery-operated space heaters, heaps of hand-stitched blankets, and their own liquor bottles. A group of them stands in a smoking circle beside a resting auger. They appear young, but Barry still wonders if he knows any of them. Their fathers perhaps. Time was he would've known each by name, where they lived. One of them kneels, his hand diving into a snow bank and reappearing with a strung sixer of canned beer.

"Just be a second, Pops," Jack, Barry's son, says, referring to the quick shoveling job he performs over the ice. The half-sized rectangular rink seems even enough for a loose eyeball job. Jack is thirty-four, an environmental lawyer, and freshly divorced. He has inherited none of Barry's physical traits—eyes like coffee saucers, all of his hair, hardly a chin at all—but also few of his personality defects. If Jack is anything, he is smart. *Never have to tell him twice,* Barry would brag to the guys at Waste Management, the company that filched thirty-seven years of his life. *Smarter than I am, and he's only seven,* then *ten,* then *seventeen.* Jack showed up unannounced just hours before with one suitcase and some kind of fire lit under his ass, of all things looking to play hockey. His first holidays alone, Barry suspects. Always the toughest. Jack is smart but also excessively sensitive, too quick to love. And like all those kids who dive in headfirst before testing the waters, he's always been the most likely to get himself hurt.

"I ain't gonna lie to you," Barry says. "I can't move around too good on these anymore."

Jack looks up from the piles of snow along his makeshift boards. "Oh that's it, huh? Throwing in the towel before we even get started?"

"Never said that." Barry reaches for one of the five sticks he and Jack dug up from behind the horde of old brown boxes in the furnace room, a dozen or so containing Vivian's things she didn't want to take with

her, empty perfume bottles and worn brassieres Barry
hadn't gotten around to throwing away. "Wouldn't get
too cocky if I were you. Your old man was quite the
sharpshooter back in his day."

"A defenseman," Jack says. He assesses his snow
removal and, satisfied, tosses his shovel aside. "You hardly
shot at all."

Jack brandishes his own stick and flips a puck to the
ice. Barry watches his son jitter across the rink, limbs
stammering, feet never quite divorcing themselves from
the step. But he's younger, his body more efficient at
picking up the slack. Barry glides behind him with grace
but he still can't match Jack's speed.

Jack has shoveled small goals on both sides; his first
shot sails far right. Barry laughs. "I'm the one should be
worried?"

"Working out the cobwebs." Jack fishes the puck from
the snow. "Just make sure you can keep up."

A wind slings down from the east, drifting dusty snow
onto their cleared rink. In an hour the sun will be gone,
its face going orange over the wooded western edge of
the lake. Barry and Vivian bought the house in '78, and
it took every cent of Barry's paycheck to maintain it. At
first it seemed worth it, spending peaceful nights and
weekends on the shoreline, fishing off the neighbor's dock
and then their own, renting a pontoon for trips to
Mickey's Steakhouse across the way. They tied a
succession of hammocks between their two towering
maples. In the early days Barry and Vivian lounged in
them together on quiet evenings and watched the
lakegoers, one-by-one, cash it in for the day. Some years
later, on hammock five or six, Vivian came out all hot
around the collar and asked if he was going to sit the

whole damn day away. Young Jack looked up from digging lakefront mud into his pail. Two years later they were divorced, Vivian moving to some city in Florida and Jack left to Barry's care.

"All right, big guy," Barry says, already feeling the hot pull of his upper thigh muscles. A demanding sport on the groin area in particular, yet in his youth he could skate for days and hardly feel a thing. "Up to seven. Face off to begin the point. Nothing's out of play until a score."

"I remember your rules, Pop," Jack says, sliding the puck to an imagined centerline. Seeing Jack huddle over the puck startles Barry: suddenly Jack is a child, unable to lug the full-sized stick he insists on playing with, his cousins and uncles letting him face off because he'll never touch the puck otherwise. Barry had hoped that after a certain time, after Jack and his cousins grew and had children of their own, they would reconstruct the old ritual, maybe even on a larger scale. A New Year's tradition perhaps. But now it's just Barry and Jack, their wives gone, their families estranged, left to play hockey one-on-one, a ridiculous notion in itself.

"On three," Jack says as Barry approaches. "Ready? One, two."

Jack drops the puck and tries to shoehorn Barry with his hips, but Barry jabs the puck away, sliding and gaining quick possession. He backs off to practice puck handling, left and right and back, but it slips away unprovoked. He'd always been better at keeping people from scoring than scoring himself. Jack pounces before Barry can recover. He slides in easily for the first score, following the puck right into the goal.

"Ha! One-nuts," he gloats, fists in the air. "Your drop, old man."

"Watch who you're calling old."

"You just called yourself that!"

"That's different," Barry says. "And don't count chickens."

Barry takes a quick brandy timeout before they hit center ice. He lets Jack control this one, sliding into defensive mode. But before he can set himself, Jack charges, wheels back and slapshoots past him into the left corner of the goal.

"The crowd goes wild!" Jack cups a hand and mimics audience cheers, skating along the boards to high-five imagined teammates. Barry retrieves the puck as his son enjoys his illusory glory. Jack loops back around and places an arm on Barry's shoulder.

"I miss this, Pop. We should've come up here more often."

"Would've had you any time."

"Terri was a homebody. Territorial. Like driving three hours was this massive inconvenience."

Barry nods. Toward the end with Vivian it had been like that with everything. Somehow each gain for Barry was her loss. Like she was heading toward a life-sized goal and anything Barry did was a jab, a check, some sort of defense against her shot at happiness. Something wouldn't work out, and it was Barry's fault even before he knew what the damn thing was.

Barry looks out onto the lake. The crowd outside the nearest shanty approaches in staggered steps, beer cans in their hands and elbow crooks.

"Would you look at this," Barry says. "Don't need to fake your crowd anymore."

As the fishermen shuffle to them, all in variegated flannel shirts and lined overalls, Barry realizes he knows none of them. They are twenty-somethings, even younger. Hardly men at all. One kid's face has three piercings that Barry can see; another wears a crooked baseball cap under his stocking hat. Back when Barry knew his lake neighbors, these kids would've been just a twinkle.

"I got five on the old man!" one of them shouts in lieu of a greeting. Jack laughs, and Barry allows the presence of this sudden and unexpected audience to goad his competitive spirit. He returns to community college, skating with his motley team in front of their small sect of hometown groupies. He feels the undeniable need to impress. And so this time after Jack drops the puck Barry hoards it. He keeps it close, leverages his body along the boards. He has gained a step, his leg and hip muscles loosening, recalling the movements he'd trained into them so long ago. The brandy runs hot in his blood. Pushing Jack left, he doubles back and veers right, opening a clear shot. Jack watches the puck with surprise, as though Barry shouldn't have such a move in him. Barry is a bit surprised himself. As the puck slides true, two of the fishermen cheer, calling the others to attention. They exchange petty wagers as Barry says to everyone, "Now we have a game."

The next few points go back and forth, Jack's initial doggedness restrained to intermittent bursts, Barry taking the game when it comes to him. At four-three Barry's left knee clicks—his bad knee, operated on numerous times in college and beyond—but at the moment he feels no pain. The fishermen applaud everything but seem generally on Barry's side, cheering for the underdog, for the long shot, which only fuels Jack's fire. He throws his body around like a child, his head down and eyes tenacious on the puck. After each score

Barry takes a soft brandy break. Jack joins him only when Barry scores.

"Damnitall," Jack says after Barry scores again, the first words besides grunts between them for some time. The crowd's whooping cheers echo off the shoreline. Wallets surface and money exchanges hands. The score is five-all.

Jack slaps the puck back to center ice. He crouches into position and gears himself for another go.

"Hold on a sec," Barry says, his body hollering at him in the brief pause. Without adrenaline his legs reap the instant, painful benefits of his youthful exertion. His ankles throb, fat in his skates, probably purpled for all the wear he's putting on them. His quads and hamstrings sear. His back, never the most reliable, holds out okay for now but he knows that clock is ticking. He goes for another brandy pull to dull away current and future pains.

"Come on. Five up," Jack says.

"Just a minute now," Barry says. "Just one goddamn minute."

"Hey, you made the rules. If you can't make it to seven. . ."

Barry leans on his stick. He knows the advantages of such spirited banter: undersized and overmatched, he often needed to rattle his opponents mentally as much as physically. "At your age," he says to Jack, "I wouldn't have let my old man score a single goal."

"Maybe. But he never would've quit."

Barry caps the brandy. "You know what's quitting? Not visiting. Not calling for a goddamn year. I'd call that quitting."

Jack's body freezes. "What do you want?" Jack lowers his voice as he spreads his thumb and pinkie into an imaginary phone. "Ah, hello Pop, Jack here. My marriage failed. I hate my job and now I have jack shit to come home to."

"If I'da known it was that bad——"

"What, you could've helped? Like I'd come to you for marriage advice."

"Watch yourself," Barry says, not lowering his voice at all.

"Drove Mom away and didn't give a damn about it. No surprise I have commitment issues."

Barry raises his stick and points it at his son. "You don't know a damn thing about me and your mother."

"Probably more than you. At least she still talks to me!"

Barry slaps his stick against the ice in reply. They stand in silence. Then a different voice, this one from the crowd: "Just kick each other's ass or drop the fucking puck already!"

Barry looks over to the kid, nineteen at best, slouched and drunker than the rest. "Go fall through some broken ice, you louse," Barry says. The kid lunges forward but a friend holds him back.

"Maybe Terri was right," Jack says. "Maybe coming here is always a mistake."

"Maybe shouldn't have then."

Jack shakes his head. But instead of stomping off as Barry expects, he moves to center ice. "You're up," he says. "Drop the damn puck."

Jack loses the face-off handily, the conversation still weighing on him. Barry moves left but then dekes opposite, gliding past a juked Jack along the right boards and backhanding a winner into the two-hole. Jack watches the puck nestle into the pile of snow. He immediately high-sticks and crashes it down, shattering the blade into pieces, splitting the shaft like a wishbone. A slice of the blade strikes Barry broadside on the leg.

"Hey!" Barry yells. "Keep your goddamned head!" Jack holds tight to his broken handle, his head skyward and eyes closed. "Okay, that's it. We're done."

"No. Grab me another stick. I'll pick this up."

"Your mom won't make this go away, Jackie Boy. She ain't been here. Since you were eight."

"Just get the stick."

Barry kicks a splintered shard to Jack's feet. "Get your own damn stick." As Jack shuffles over, Barry adds, "You know, that stick was older than you." Jack bends, pauses, then dons his new stick. He encircles the ring, avoiding Barry's eyes. "You gonna keep your head?"

Jack flicks the last of his former stick from the rink. "Six-five," He says.

Jack easily wins the face-off. Barry's legs and back seize on him, stiffened from the break. He hobbles back to defend. Jack surges with speed—finally gliding, finally letting the skates do their work—and Barry knows he can't match it, not without pulling a muscle, maybe worse. Jack shimmies as he easily hits the empty netter. The flannelled fisherman don't cheer the goal, their betting giving way to the escalated family drama unfurling before them.

"There it is," Jack says. "Sixes. Next goal takes all."

Barry handles the next face-off with no intention of giving Jack a shot at the puck. He levels his hip and grinds forward, leveraging his body for position. Jack prods at his feet, jabs him with his stick, trying to break Barry's bull rush down. He sends a cheap butt-end shot to Barry's ribs and pilfers the puck.

Barry's adrenaline kicks in and ignites his muscles. He knows what it's like to play angry; hell, he'd spent a good deal of his high school years pissed off without much reason. So even though Jack now has the puck, Barry knows Jack's rage will lead to a mistake. Will cause him to lose control. Jack handles back and forth but then he surges forward too quickly, the puck shooting out in front of him. A gliding gift, as easy a pick as a natural born defender can ask for. Barry flicks the puck between Jack's feet. In haste Jack flings his stick backward and entangles his legs in the process. He trips flat on his stomach, leaving Barry with a clean breakaway.

Barry hustles anyway, taking nothing for granted, gearing up for the uncontested game-winner. Just before winding up he looks over his shoulder and glimpses his son, head down to the ice, shoulders sunk low. The look of a man who knows he's lost.

Barry slows up and flicks his wrist, sending the puck across the ice. It slides over ice chips and snow dust and lands dead-center in the goal.

Barry looks to the crowd, which has unceremoniously begun to disperse. Jack remains down, his arms and legs splayed like a struck deer, his nose to the ice. When he does rise his gaze remains outward, beyond the trekking fishermen to the middle of the lake.

"Good game, Jackie Boy," Barry says.

"You know what, Pop? Fuck off." In one motion Jack dispenses his stick and gloves. He stomps toward the shore like someone new to the ice.

"Christ Almighty, you still a sore loser?"

"I actually thought—" Jack says to the shore. "I thought it'd be nice to see you again. Even thought you might, just might, have a little sympathy."

"Sympathy? Sympathy I got. Letting you win isn't part of that deal. Not when you get outplayed."

"Win. Lose. Do you know any other language?"

"What? I've had it," Barry says. "Next time you need sympathy call your goddamn mother."

Jack doesn't reply. He tromps through the yard to his Jetta. Without taking off his skates he enters and shuts the door. Barry waits for the ignition to fire, for headlights and a jerky reversal, but Jack just sits, hands at his sides, eyes on the frozen lake as the sun disappears behind the western treetops. At the closest shanty, the drunk fisherman unzips his fly and pisses in their direction, right on the open ice.

"To hell with it," Barry says. "With all of you." Then he goes inside.

Half an hour of local news and two brandys later Barry rises to the window. Jack's car is still there, Jack inside motionless, probably freezing his ass off. No different when he was a kid, hiding under the basement stairs in a nook only he could access. The first time he'd sat so stone silent Barry couldn't find him; Vivian panicked and called the police. From then on they always knew where to look, and to send Vivian, only Vivian, to coax him out.

Barry makes spaghetti. His body argues against its every move; his shoulders pinch and his back whines. It's been years since he's done more than a brisk walk. Each sip of brandy snakes down his throat and flushes him with temporary relief, but soon enough he needs another. He watches the water to a boil, then the dried noodles soften and bend. He prepares two large plates and digs immediately into his. His goddamned stubborn son. He eats intemperately, pasta dangling from his mouth, red sauce strewing about his face. When he finishes his own plate he slides it aside and pulls the other to him. "Sit out there all night for all I care," he says, shoveling his fork into Jack's plate as well. He eats every noodle to the last.

When Barry stands from the table his legs seize. He nearly keels over, saved only by grabbing the chair he just vacated. When his legs finally unlock he stutters his way across the living room only to see Jack right where he left him. "Go on then. Get out of here!" he says to the window. Though Jack could never hear him, at that moment he turns from the lake as though he has. "Fine. Just goddamn fine."

Barry turns the TV volume louder than necessary. The screen appears fuzzed even when he squints, the brandy and pasta hitting him all at once. He should have made some coffee, or gotten a soda from the fridge. Within minutes he is out.

Barry wakes to Jack's face hovering over him. It is dark. Jack has turned the TV off but no lights on. Barry's whole body feels battered; he'd been in fights before, and aside from the centralization of the bruises and pain, this pretty much feels the same. Jack's arms reach around Barry's torso, and though Barry wants to resist, his body will have none of it. A midnight wind cascades against the house as Jack whispers, "I've got you, Pop. I've got you."

Jack shimmies beneath one of Barry's shoulders. Barry gains footing but can only take hobbled, baby-like steps. His left knee screams at him with each lunge. Jack bears him through the living room. "Almost there," Jack says at his bedroom door. When they reach the bed Barry expects to crash down upon it, but Jack rests him down as careful as a parent with a newborn.

"Pop?" Jack says.

"Yeah, Jackie Boy?"

"Maybe use a bib next time."

Barry gives a pained laugh. Jack closes the door behind him. Half-asleep, Barry stares at the door for minutes, expecting his five-year-old son to careen through it, the Saturday morning sun following him in. Vivian would make sliver dollar pancakes; Barry would remain in bed for another hour, the smell of browned batter and coffee drifting into his light sleep. He hadn't appreciated then what a wonderful thing it is to hear someone moving around your house when you wake. Now he hears, above the wind slapping his vinyl siding, his adult son's footsteps on the kitchen hardwood, on the foyer tile, then the squeal of the front door opening and the desolate click as it closes behind him.

Intimations of Chloe

She hates her father. For some reason it seems important for Jasmine to say at that moment, sitting across from Pandl with his beady eyes and his new, lotion-shined, Chinese-script tattoo on his neck. The eyes harden, soften, harden again. His moods vacillate just so simply. Jasmine shifts to the menu, to sandwiches with slices of avocado and sprouts, to vanilla lattes, to crepes and biscottis, to laundry-lists of exotic teas. Pluot green. Cinnamon Earl Grey. White baneberry. Isn't that poisonous? She orders it.

"You do this," Pandl says. "Intentionally play the victim. Poor fucking Jas."

"You're not going to order anything?"

"Place is garbage. Your sandwiches are better." He scratches at the tattoo. "Why are you doing this? Why now?"

Jasmine doesn't have an answer. An angular woman and her bearded lover at the next table discuss with enthusiasm their pending trip to Target Field. A middle-aged woman enters in white gloves, a dark purebred golden retriever at each foot, the left one's face grayed around the eyes and up the cheeks, its ribs paltry, its steps measured. Not long for the world. The young one trounces to the corner bamboo palm and lifts its leg. The white-gloved woman slides her arms in disapproving akimbo as though the dog will understand. Six months earlier, Pandl's German Shepherd Chloe choked herself to death in the tiny backyard behind his townhome. She was trying to get at the neighbor kids who for years had dangled sandwich meats just out of her reach and pelted her with snowballs. When he sees the goldens, Pandl's face jowls into intimations of Chloe, just like the first time he and Jasmine met which was, coincidentally, at a Twins matinee. A mutual friend introduced them. Pandl's shirt was mustard-stained, Jasmine's tied at her waist, their sunglasses evenly, absurdly large. Jasmine didn't know whether to shake his hand or just wave, and so in the awkward process knocked his peanuts to the ground. Picking them up together, Pandl looked at Jasmine with those same eyes, hangdog and wistful. They had a common interest in carnivals but enjoyed them for different reasons. He paid for dinners and the sex was tolerable. His first name sounded exotic enough to piss off her parents in phone calls home. She invented increasingly absurd lies about him at the expense of Herb in particular—he was a diehard Vikings fan, a pushy vegan, a practicing Hindu temple priest. But she must admit she has grown tired of the façade. She must acknowledge that Pandl is not her rebellion, nor is he her father. He is, in fact, nothing.

Pandl returns from the restroom with a paper towel still in his hands. "Why do complete strangers think it's okay to talk in the john?"

"You have one of those faces."

"I do not." He eyes the paper towel with interest, as though surprised to see it. "I don't want any type of face." "Sometimes it doesn't matter what we want."

A father laughs too loudly at something his daughter says. When Jasmine's tea arrives, Pandl unscrews the saltshaker and pours in every last granule. Then comes the crying, in front of everyone, as though they are sitting in his smoke-filled kitchen with the blinds closed. He lets the tears, the twin trails of snot, drape his face. He makes fists on the table and asks the crooked ceiling fan, "Where did we go wrong?"

Jasmine doesn't know where to begin.

Margerie's Concerto

To Margerie's mind, her life began on a day just before her seventeenth birthday. It was winter. Her mother Claire donned the bench of their baby grand piano with stick-straight posture, a certain sign of a foul mood. Margerie hesitantly joined her, placing a light, summery concerto on the desk that Claire slapped away. Since being let go from her job a year earlier, Claire had taken more and more to the painkillers that triggered extremes both lethargic and fiery. When she wasn't excoriating Margerie, she spent long afternoons in her bedroom with blinds closed and pillows over her head. She audibly wept. After these spells she would emerge and apologize, hugging Margerie fiercely. This cycle repeated itself, and though the duration of its seasons changed, Margerie knew this slap of the concerto was only the start of their winter.

Margerie sat up as well, already taller than Claire and still growing, as Claire slid Chopin onto the desk. Margerie knew she ought to say nothing, to play Claire's implacable demands with tactful precision. But what of Margerie's own moods? Was she not allowed an opinion? Couldn't she too seethe with the volcano-like vitriol that rose in her mother for no reason?

So Margerie impudently played the Chopin, jumpy one measure, sluggish the next. When Claire plunked an imperious finger down on the highest note, as she always did when Margerie made a mistake, Margerie ignored it. Margerie reached to flip a page and Claire seized hold of her hand.

"You're playing like an adolescent."

Margerie looked down at her mother, at the sallow cheekbones and reddish hair already streaked with full strands of white. At her wizened body seemingly shrinking with age. Margerie wondered what, if any, traits she had inherited from this woman.

"Start over," Claire said.

"What's the point?"

"The point?" Claire looked at Margerie with a puzzled expression, as though she had just asked about life's deepest quandaries, about death or God or love.

"I don't play for anyone but you anyway."

"That will change."

"When?"

But Claire didn't answer. Her eyes roamed out the window, to the trio of plum trees in their backyard to which, come harvest time, Claire would devote her fervent attentions. Margerie sighed. "I'm done with—"

But then Claire redoubled her grip on Margerie's hand, sending a shrill of pain up her arm. Instinctively Margerie wrested her arm back but was met with an even harsher pull. She marveled only a moment at the surprising strength of her mother before her free hand slipped across the lid and her head crashed into the piano, the resounding mash of keys flashing into her ear just before she lost consciousness.

After two days Claire took Margerie to the hospital in Marinette. They sat side-by-side for an hour under the clinical lights of the waiting room. Margerie watched another mother read her toddler daughter a Dr. Seuss book. Beside them a farmer, kicked by his own heifer, tried in vain to conceal the pink, tender flesh dangling like snot from his nostril. In the examination room, Claire recounted to the doctor a fabricated story of Margerie slipping on ice and colliding with a tree. The doctor asked simple questions Margerie heard as though through a hollow tube. She felt groggy, yes. Had trouble concentrating. And pain, palpable pain, more piercing than dull, particularly on the right side. She drifted into light-filled dreams during a CT scan. The doctor determined that overall she would be fine, but that she had lost all hearing in her right ear. Temporarily at least, and possibly forever.

A month later, near Christmas, Margerie set off. Claire had capped her dinner with the remainder of her prescription and would stay in bed all night. And so Margerie simply opened their patio door, walked through their backyard and the thin canopy of trees behind, wending the quarter mile of snow-covered woods all the way to the icy shores of Lake Noquebay.

She stepped out onto the frozen lake, dropped to her knees and wiped away a layer of fresh snow that glimmered crystalline in the starlight, not minding that much of it burned on her hands and wrists. The water along the shoreline was gently frozen and smooth as piano keys. She created a swept path as she ventured farther, staring as a child might into a snow globe, seeing one stagnant, beautiful vision in hopes it would come to life. In a sudden flash of her future she imagined standing on this lake in ten, twenty, fifty years. A twenty-something turned middle-aged turned elderly. She saw her entire life this way, both embraced and strangled, beloved and arrested. She saw in the opaque ice the vast, incalculable number of lives she would never lead.

When she rose the ice suddenly cracked and, with a single breath, Noquebay pulled her under.

She landed in a shock of cold. She scrambled to rise. When she regained her feet, however, the water reached only to her thighs. She plodded out of the lake and into the trees, her hands clenched to her chest, pants clinging to her calves. As the snow and dead leaves crunched under her hobbling feet, she thought not of how cold she was but of how angry her mother would be. How she would never let Margerie go. Margerie dashed through her backyard and past the hibernating plum trees, her lungs incensed from the winter air, and into her house.

Her hands were numb. Her shoes would not relinquish her feet. In her bedroom she stripped her frosting clothes and shoved them into a clandestine corner of her closet. As she emerged, naked and shivering, she heard her door open. There stood her mother, unexpectedly awake. Her eyes were alarmingly alert.

"I wanted a bath," Margerie said, surprised at the swiftness of her believable lie. Claire gave an incredulous look. But then she just shook her head in exhaustion and returned to her room. Margerie soaked in the tub until the water went lukewarm, feeling the prickle of a fever and altogether more alive than she'd ever felt before.

Margerie didn't recognize Claire's full decline into herself until late summer. She spent more time in her room, wasting away entire days, and her pallid body shriveled even more. But then she skipped the first days of the plum harvest, and Margerie knew that some invisible divide had been crossed. That her fall had reached a terminal velocity. For Margerie's entire life, whenever the fingernail-sized white buds in mid-summer turned to fist-sized fruit in early autumn, Claire would pluck each one from its sagging limb with devotion. Year after year Claire collected, taking her time, spending entire afternoons. It seemed the one thing that could truly mollify her, body and mind. In Margerie's magnanimous moods she offered to help, and Claire rewarded her by sharing memories of her father. He was handsome and devilishly charming, two traits that seemed to pair together without fail. Tall like Margerie. At some point he worked for nearly every company in Crivitz, a testament either to his utility or to his languorous inability to hold a job, even Claire didn't know which. He poured preternatural efforts into courting Claire, impregnated her, and then foolishly manned a lift on a day with torrential winds. He of course fell, and died a day later of complications. If only he had survived to shoulder some of the burden, Claire would say. If he had been around, her chronic back problems that germinated with the pregnancy wouldn't have sprouted through a child-carrying adolescence, wouldn't have blossomed in her laborious work at Thiel farm. She wouldn't wake every single morning to stabbing, paralyzing pain. Things would be different. In those moments, Claire looked at Margerie with something akin to love, a look with faint whispers of what might have been but never could be.

But now the plums ripened and still Claire didn't move from her room. She ate from jars of canned fruit or not at all. She called to Margerie only to chastise her. Margerie watched hours of game shows and soap operas, tinkered simple children's tunes on the piano, and the trees' thin branches drooped under the weight of nascent fruit that eventually fell and split on the ground. Within days, fat plums circled the trees, their skins rent and insides leaking like festering wounds.

And then the next morning, lifting her good ear from her pillow, Margerie heard a soft drone outside. She peered out her window to see overripe fruit dropping like hail to the ground. Underneath, amidst the plum carrion, swarmed legions of bees.

They were everywhere. In awe, Margerie stepped out back and watched them loop and throng. She could hardly see the fruit for the packs that flew with an odd sense of community. It was almost beautiful. She took another step, apparently one too close, because a group recognized her intrusion on their feast and ambushed. They stung her a dozen times before she could slam the door and twice more when she tried to shake them from her hair. Her body stippled with red, pulsating mounds, Margerie realized that her mother had harvested all those years not just out of some strange labor of love for plums but out of necessity. That her mother's life, like her own, reamined tethered to this painfully inescapable house.

After all it is easy, uneventful, the day she once again wanders free, this time out her front door. It is early afternoon. The week-long headaches and irritations of the bee stings are nearly gone. She thinks just to reach the end of their dirt driveway, awaiting her mother's voice like a tracking dog at her heels. But she hears nothing. She continues on.

The woods around her rustle in an autumn wind. Jack pines and maples line the road. She tunes her good ear to the distinct calls of robins and chickadees. The gravel beneath her feet grumbles just before cars dart past, some giving her plenty of space, others buzzing dangerously close. She realizes how unfamiliar these roads are to her; she hits many culs-de-sac and must turn around. She has no idea the distance she's traveled. But as the wind accelerates it carries a feeling of providence: that this walk, the events of this day, are somehow preordained. That if she just abandons control to fate, this clairvoyant world will lead her. The wind guides her hand up, extends her hitchhiker's thumb to the empty road. She waits. And within a minute, a car arrives over the next hill and slows beside her.

It is a young man, thirties, darkly tanned on his face and forearms. He wears sunglasses and a bandanna of the American flag over his head. Tied to the rack of his small Volkswagen SUV is an oversized buck, its hind legs draped down the back window, clearly obstructing his view. He rolls down his window and asks, "Where you headed?"

"Just into town."

He nods Margerie over to the passenger side, and before she can buckle her seatbelt they are off.

They take the coiling corners fast, too fast: he seems to trust the ostensible emptiness of the roads. The deer slides and flops against its tenuous rope constraints. He seems uninterested in conversation, saying only "Hope you don't mind" as he cracks his window and lights a menthol cigarette. He knows the lyrics to songs on every station, country and rock and pop, but has the vexing habit of cutting every song short. When he scans to a classical station playing Bruch she reaches to stay his hand. His skin is abrasive, the nails untrimmed. He looks to her for the first time.

"A classic lover, huh," he says, putting his right hand on the wheel for the first time. "Sure thing."

Her touch has opened him up, has given him permission to commence the deer story he wants to tell. Two solitary days in the woods, he says with pride, without spotting even a raccoon. His brother and father throw in the towel the night before, giving in to the brandy and still asleep in the morning when he treks out by himself, deep into the woods, farther than he's ever gone. Unlucky stand, unlucky land, whatever's keeping him from seeing a single goddamn thing needs to change. Halfway to lunch, halfway in a dream, he hears the buck trounce just on the other side of the tree. Just struts right by, cock of the walk. So close he's afraid to even breathe. So he's got one shot, but he'll have to whip around and fire all in one, the thing will bolt on first sound. He holds his breath, prays to a God he doesn't really believe in. His heart pounds in his ears. And then whip boom, his bow clean through the heart, ace in the hole. Had to track fifty yards tops. But the thing, as Margerie can see, is huge. And he's out deep, all alone. Doesn't know if he can leave it and find his way back before dark. So what else can he do but drag the thing, all two hundred pounds easy, through jagged woods and back to his brother's house. He can't tell her how much of a bitch the woods really are, you never know until you got to lug something like that by yourself. This baby's going up on the wall, her driver says, and not just because it's a fourteen pointer. A story to tell the kids one day, that's for sure, if he ever gets around to having any.

He lights a second cigarette from the dying embers of the first. They turn onto a road familiar to Margerie and soon reach town. They pass an abandoned tavern, a skinning and tanning business. Margerie eyes the familiar billboards for stump removal and the only lawyer in town. They pass Mo's, the one restaurant Claire took Margerie to with any regularity, and she realizes how deeply her festering disdain for her confinement to her mother's care, to this small town, has blinded her to the small things. How little appreciation she can muster. They reach the first stoplight, just a few blocks from Main Street. He turns to her.

"Where you headed exactly?"

The only places she can conjure are the restaurant they just passed, the school, the grocery. She veers him left and continues turn-by-turn directions until they near the end of the business district.

"A friend's house or something?"

Margerie has no answer. Her driver pulls to the curb, cuts short the Bruch. He removes his sunglasses.

"You gotta help me. I'm not from around here."

"I think—" she begins. "I think I'm running away."

Margerie is surprised by her own avowal. It settles on her driver's body heavily, like a cascading mound of snow. But then he nods, the pieces of their peculiar drive falling into place. He lets out a soft laugh.

"I don't suppose you're eighteen." When Margerie shakes her head he says, "You at least want to tell me why?"

In his eyes she sees his reluctance, his sympathies fighting against the realization that he shouldn't abet her, that he endangers himself by doing so.

"You know the last thing I did before picking you up?" he says. "Told my dad to go fuck himself. Can't spend five minutes in the same room anymore."

"My father died when I was very young."

He nods again, as though her father's perilous death is the only way her life could have been. And perhaps it is. Perhaps everything, big and small, has conspired to get Margerie here. If that is true, where will she be tomorrow?

"And your mom?" he asks.

For the first time since her driveway Margerie thinks of Claire, lying prostrate on her bed, her body withering and lucidity fleeting. At what point would she realize Margerie was gone? What would she do? Would she pour her sometimes dogged labor into searching for her? Or would Margerie, like the plums, simply become one of the many things Claire allowed to slip from her grasp, another of life's castaways, abandoned to the weight of her addiction?

"Look, honey," her driver says. "You don't have to tell me. But I do think I should level with you. You have no bag. Probably no money. Seems to me you haven't thought this through. And it's not easy to just up and run away. Not nowadays anyhow."

A semi-truck rattles the SUV as it passes, kicking into the side a small symphony of gravel. A car coming opposite flickers its headlights. In the driver's conflicting mind, one side of the argument wins out and he ignites his engine, whips an abrupt U-turn and heads back through town. They retrace Margerie's misguided path back in the direction they came, back toward Claire and the lake and Margerie's small, small world.

But then the engine drops as he slows and pulls into the Pines Motel. Its parking lot is little more than an extended driveway along a stretch of six rooms and a lobby. He pulls next to the only other vehicle, a rusted-out truck with two jet skis attached on a faultless trailer. He enters the lobby and Margerie exits the Volkswagen. The low timbre of cicadas has begun its nightly opus. Her driver returns minutes later with a room key attached to a miniature oar. She looks at the key, at the worn grooves in the oar's wood, years upon years of engraved palms and thumbs.

"You've got until noon tomorrow. Do me a favor? Sleep on it. You'll know what to do then."

Before leaving he leans close, places a hand on her shoulder and whispers something into her bad ear. The words are indistinct but behind them, somewhere in their core, rests a low resonance that echoes onto her eardrum. The beginning of a sound. His smile is genuine as he returns to his deer-adorned SUV and drives away.

Margerie watches him go with the acute certainty that she will never see him again. They hadn't even exchanged names. At the door to room four, she fights the key inside its lock but then stops. She realizes that, excepting television, she's never before seen the inside of a motel room. She imagines dated lamps, besmeared carpeting, a floral pattern bedspread, all tinted brown. Dead flies in the bathtub. The curtains will smell of Claire's plum jams, of her empty, dusted pill bottles. In the coming years, as early as tomorrow perhaps, she will spend lonely nights in places like this. But not tonight.

She lets go, the oar jangling on its chain, and watches the sun set luminous over the wooded west. Then she walks down the driveway, to the road and into town, where she knows another windswept traveler will bear her burdens. He will take her clear of town this time, in any direction so long as it's away, far away, until her life resembles nothing of her mother, of plums and pills, of Crivitz itself. She will forsake the classics and instead write her own concerto, a harmonious symphony replete with air and light and jazzy improvisation, with an abundance of voluminous, vulnerable, beautiful room to grow.

Encyclopedia Helenica

1 **48.6 lbs.:** Weight of Helen Trudeau on 1 November 2016, taken on locker room scale in Crivitz High School, an official, sliding-metal physician scale that bobs and ticks and leaves Helen in unnecessary suspense waiting for the thing to sink down, to become heavier than her, sliding past 130, her presumed weight, it has been that long since she's stepped on a scale or even thought about it, 135, 140, no, 145, no no no, for the love of Christ don't make her slide it all the way back and lug the big weight to 150, until finally it stops.

Helen: (Greek, "Shining Light") 16 July 1999–Present. Of Crivitz, Wisconsin, born and raised. Teenage female of slightly-below-average stature (5' 1" at last doctor's visit) and above-average weight (see *148.6 lbs.*). Vice-president of Crivitz High School drama club. Fun-loving only child of Trent and Elise Trudeau who finds adventure in everyday situations (see *Helen's Dominant Behaviors and Traits, pre-1 November 2016*).

Golden Burger: Restaurant chain with seven locations in northeast Wisconsin; Crivitz location frequented often

during open lunch period by Helen and best friend/
confidante Gina.

Geez Hel, hungry are we?: Words spoken from Gina in
a brash but ultimately enlightening tone (see *Gina's
Dominant Behaviors and Traits*), the first reason for Helen's
instantaneous and repulsive realization that she has
demolished her entire meal before Gina has put even a
dent in hers.

**Haphazard remains of a Third-Pound Golden Cheesy
Burger with fries, lettuce and tomato discarded in a
slovenly mix of ketchup and mayonnaise:** Second reason.

Crivitz, Wisconsin: 1883–Present. Founded by German
immigrant Frederick John Bartels; subsequently named
for former German hometown. Located at 45°14′2″N
88°0′25″W, Wisconsin, United States of America. Small
village of approximately 990 people (2010 Census).
Current graduating high school class of 28. Largest of
the small townships and municipalities surrounding Lake
Noquebay.

Gina: (English, diminutive form of Georgina, feminine
version of George, "Land worker") 19 September 1999–
Present. Of Crivitz, Wisconsin, born and raised. Teenage
girl average in both height and weight, not exactly thin
but not heavy either, certainly not in comparison to present
company.

Drizella, the tawdrier of the two Wicked Stepsisters:
Helen's casted role in Crivitz High School Players'
production of *Cinderella* (see *Helen's Acting Resume*), cast

beside Gina as Anastasia, their on-stage chemistry and off-stage shenanigans a contributing factor in casting decision by Mrs. Bing, music teacher and play director.

Fifteenth rehearsal, delving into "Lovely Night" scene, a showcase for the stepsisters and a chance for Helen to really shine: Helen's extracurricular activity on 1 November 2016.

Helen's Heart[1]: Just not in it, a fact noted verbally by both Gina and Mrs. Bing.

Hey, forget what I said earlier. See you tomorrow, okay?: Gina's conciliatory words before she drops Helen off at home.

One helping of turkey, minimal gravy; small scoop of mashed potatoes; slice of white bread, buttered; glass of milk, subsequently rinsed out and refilled with water: Helen's dinner on 1 November 2016, the first time she scrutinizes the amounts of what she eats in lieu of how her body feels.

You feeling okay, dear?: Question posed from Elise to Helen at dinner table.

Elise: (Greek, "Pledged to God") 23 December 1970– Present. Of Crivitz, Wisconsin, neither born nor raised. Wife of Trent Trudeau for 19+ years. Woman of medium height and above-average build, plump but not fat, not really, a typical mom body, though Helen notices unhealthy extra folds on her upper arms, off-putting way her stomach rests limply over jeans.

I'm fine. Just don't have much of an appetite tonight: Helen's timid response, followed by a haste placing of her plate in dishwasher and retreating to her bedroom, her stomach smarting with a lack of fullness, but then maybe that's not it, maybe she is full, maybe fullness is a relative term that she has accustomed herself to, maybe thin people experience it differently.

149.2 lbs.: Weight of Helen Trudeau on night of 1 November 2016, taken on scale in quaint adjacent bathroom, painted pink and a bit girlish for a seventeen-year-old, she's now noticing.

The Mirror: 53.5 in. x 17.5 in. over-the-door body-length mirror with silver double-beaded frame, made by Reflections Mirror and Glass Company, in front of which Helen stands in her bedroom.

Lucky Brand Bootleg Princess Jeans, size 6[1]: Helen's old favorites, ones that hugged her hips and flared flatteringly at the leg, that now won't even pull up over her thighs, how big those thighs are, holy hell, what has she done to herself.

You're a growing girl: Previous justification, accepted as fact by Helen—as she has done with most parental truisms, hers being the good parents they generally are—given intermittently by Trent and Elise as to why her favorite clothes no longer fit.

That bullshit: What, standing in front of The Mirror, pants desperately around thighs, Helen sees right through.

Skipping breakfast: An idea with nothing but negative connotations (see *Most Important Meal of the Day!*), counter-weighted by Helen's following justifications:

1. Simple math, read by Helen in some health magazine once, stating that to lose one pound of fat in a week, she need excise 200 calories from her daily diet and burn 200 more in exercise (see *Common Weight Loss Misconceptions*),
2. Lunch is only +/- four hours away, and
3. She's not really hungry anyway.

One pound a week: Lofty but, Helen expects, reasonable goal, considering all the excess weight she has to lose (see multiple entries for *Overweight*).

Renee's ass[1]: First thing Helen notices in the hall morning of 2 November 2017; the ass Helen used to have not so long ago, freshman year even, the ass that caught glances, particularly in Lucky Brand Bootleg Princess Jeans, size 6, ass that filled but didn't stretch pants, didn't tuck into itself, didn't fold over underwear, just didn't didn't didn't.

Xander: (diminuitive form of Alexander, Greek, "Defender of Men") (*See also Helen's Perpetual Love Object*) 17 November 1999–Present. Teenage male of uncanny good looks, like a Greek god himself, body sculpted from three-sport varsity activity, biceps and pectorals in particular, chiseled as if from stone; hair dark brown and curled just so over ears, enticingly disheveled; eyes a deep, lose-yourself-in-them brown as well; and smile, God his smile, you should see him smile.

Prince Charming: Role of Xander York in *Cinderella,* naturally.

Body Blast of Crivitz: Gym that Helen frequents immediately after play practice on 2 November 2016, it being the only workout option outside of high school exercise facility, but there's no chance (see *Never, Nuh-Uh, Fat Chance, When Pigs Fly,* and *Not in a Million Years*) of her working out there, wearing her mom's tight-fitting yoga pants and tank top that are incapable of containing her body, fat folding over the arm holes and in strange creases behind her legs, nope, not until she fixes this.

Body Blast, contents: Eight newer, shining silver treadmills; five exercise bikes; three elliptical machines; two Stairmasters; one outdated rowing machine, rope tattered, placed in far corner to further discourage use; weight benches with bars, plates; long rows of free weights; medicine balls of all sizes; resistance cords; front desk with young attendant in hot-orange shirt; patrons of all body types, from the thin and beautiful to the robust and ugly; three walls of floor-to-ceiling mirrors mirrors mirrors.

1.62 miles: Distance Helen manages to run-walk-run in unsystematic sequence before her throat burns with bile and her gelatin legs threaten entire shutdown (see *Exercise Side Effects, Negative*).

To discuss a new exercise plan: Helen's presumptive reason for visit to Dr. Samson on 5 November 2016.

To gauge how bad she's really gotten: Helen's actual reason.

Overweight[1]: (see also *Fatty, Pear-Shaped, Obeast, Lard Ass, Buffet Slayer, Piggy,* and *Wisconsin Skinny*) Classification, based on body mass index (BMI), calculated with a basic equation of height and weight, of large percentage of American adult men and women.

28.5: Helen's BMI, not just Overweight but hovering nauseatingly close to the next highest classification, Obese, and which Doctor Samson assures her can be a natural part of growing, really this measure is for adults and not a terrific one at that, not something Helen should be too concerned about as long as she's active, but if she likes she could drink more water, exercise a bit more, for Doctor Samson it's really about life choices, you see, about starting healthy habits that will lead to good decisions when older, those are the types of successes she sees, not those who live in the extremes.

I understand: Helen's only verbal response during visit.

147.7 lbs.: Weight of Helen on 8 November 2016, after intense, fatigue-inducing first week of exercise and diet, not nearly enough weight loss to justify pain and ascetic self-flagellation, causing seething self-doubt and a desire to quit in Helen (see *Helen's Dominant Behaviors and Traits, post-1 November 2016*).

Back on the horse: Where Helen gets the next day at Body Blast.

DO YOU REALLY WANT THIS?: Mantra Helen develops while stretching 2 miles into 2.5, pushing beyond burn and bile and yearning to just give up.

Killed two and a half miles today at Body Blast! And that's just the start!: Helen's Facebook status 9 November 2016, her first post in eighty-three days, liked or otherwise emojied by ten friends within minutes, then sixteen, some responses adorned with encouraging remarks from random classmates, from great-aunt Clarissa she has never met in person, from Gina.

Julia's Calorie Bible: Book bought by Helen at Marinette Barnes & Noble to prove devotion to mantra, containing calorie counts for every food Helen has ever eaten, the cover flaunting Julia's flawless body, her endorsement reading *This book contains the information you need to live a healthy, natural lifestyle. I guarantee it will work!*, her smile so gargantuan it can only be real.

1,025: Calories in a Third-Pound Golden Cheesy Burger with fries, a number Helen reluctantly looks up with equal proportions shame and disgust.

Eight glasses a day: Generic recommendation for intake of water (see *Common Weight Loss Misconceptions*) which is the least Helen can do, as water occupies the stomach and is the healthiest thing, really, for her.

Daily Schedule, 10 November 2016: (see similar entries for 11, 12, and 13 November 2016; week of 16 November; most weekdays thereafter leading up to *Cinderella* performance, minus Thanksgiving, 30 November and 6 December [see also *Pathetic Days Helen WILL Put Behind Her*])

1. Wake up
2. Skip breakfast
3. Coast through morning classes, paying attention only in Pre-Calc to impress Xander York (see *Helen's Perpetual Love Object*)
4. Lunch: turkey sandwich plain, apple and/or banana, granola bar, water
5. Dream about Xander during afternoon classes
6. Play practice
7. Body Blast baby!
8. Post workout update to Facebook
9. Dinner: half plate of whatever Elise makes, less if thick on carbs or sauces
10. Immediately catalogue from Julia's Calorie Bible, down to the crumb, day's food intake, drawing a hard double-line underneath to keep from eating more.

Eating $\leq$ three hours before bed: Kiss of death, as Helen has read that such calories store immediately as excess fat (see *Common Weight Loss Misconceptions*).

132.0 lbs.: Weight of Helen Trudeau on 1 January 2017, day nationally known for resolutions of the weight variety (see *Make a new you!* and *You're only fooling yourself*).

No need for resolutions when the resolve is already there!: Helen's Facebook post on 1 January 2017, recipient of the highest number of likes she's ever received, 212, accompanied by selfie on treadmill at Body Blast, most machines behind her empty, considering.

Overweight[2]: Helen still, at 25.7, according to the BMI image Helen has Googled and downloaded as her laptop wallpaper, replacing old movie image of Hugh Jackman's aching, above-average turn as Jean Valjean in Hollywood adaptation of *Les Misérables.*

Lucky Brand Bootleg Princess Jeans, size 6[2]: Still-unfitting jeans that simultaneously affirm BMI's correctness and Helen's resolve.

Granola bar; one glass orange juice; four slices whole grain wheat bread, two on sandwich and two toasted, unbuttered; three slices shaved turkey; one slice reduced-fat cheddar cheese; Cortland apple; medium-sized banana; bagel with cream cheese; can store-bought chicken noodle soup; two squares Hershey's milk chocolate bar: Full caloric intake for 5 January 2017, just under 1,200. Minimum amount of food Helen figures she can consume, an assumption she discovers in weeks subsequent to be untrue.

Third-pound Golden Cheesy Burger with fries: All Helen can think about during *Cinderella* dress rehearsal.

How her Drizella costume still hugs her torso and hips, this repugnant dress that should droop wickedly, she should look comedic in it, a thin girl in abnor-mally baggy clothes but all she looks is fat, why would a Prince Charming ever want this: All Helen can think about during *Cinderella* performances (seven) the week of

8-14 January 2017, causing lackluster performance and abundance of stink-eyes from Gina.

Drizella's Fat Foot: Reason why Prince Charming cannot, with much exaggerated force, cram glass slipper onto Cinderella's stepsister, even after much finagling by Wicked Stepmother, confirming Drizella's falsity as love object in question on previous night's escapades.

Helen's own disgusting, disturbingly obtuse Fat Foot: Why Helen cannot enjoy her only scene with Xander, her chance to really turn it on but there he is, on his knee in front of her, hand grasping the Fat Foot, face so convincingly horrified his disgust can only be real.

Helen's Heart[2]: Beaten, bruised, battered, trampled and stomped on, broken but hopefully not beyond repair (see *DO YOU REALLY WANT THIS?*).

Going to the gym again?: Elise's question posed to Helen after final Sunday matinee performance.

Yep: Helen's terse reply.

Okay, but come right home after. Dad's making pot roast. Now that the play's over, I was thinking we should get back to family dinners: Elise's earnest and softly spoken plea to Helen, her common matronly speech pattern (see *Elise's Dominant Behaviors and Traits*) that makes her both more endearing and easier to ignore.

Hey, Helen. You look great today: Helen's first verbal compliment on her newly formed body, delivered in school by Vince Belfast, underclassman from *Cinderella* chorus to whom she has never spoken, to whom she has never before given a second thought.

Yeah, thanks: Helen's abject reply, the compliment itselfnot carrying the inspirational heft it should, not validating treadmill hours upon hours, knee aches and near-constant fatigue (see *Exercise Side Effects, Negative*), because shouldn't the bigger fish be noticing by now, shouldn't someone from cast, shouldn't Xander.

Death[1]: Inevitable end of life, reached by many due to unfortunate and unforeseen early circumstances (see *Before His/Her Time*), by others under more expected and lengthy but no less unfortunate circumstances (see *Lived a Full Life*), that this realization feels like.

Exercise Side Effects, Negative: Abdominal cramping; wheezing; dizziness bordering on fainting; sweating, amounts ranging from minute to excessive, so much that body excretes salt on shoulders; significant pain in the ass; shin splints; near-constant fatigue; bile burning up throat; acid dripping into stomach; papery, wafer-like feeling of arms and legs; knee aches; going on and on so much that body, with little else to do, convulses and threatens entire shutdown.

Exercise Side Effects, Positive: Relatively less self-loathing; pleasant disappearance of monthly period; loss of appetite; relatively less blubber under fingers while pinching; reduced bowel movements.

120.0 lbs.: Weight of Helen Trudeau on 9 February 2017.

Overweight[3]: No longer Helen's classification on BMI scale, now sliding into Optimal range, though still just below the line at 24, not far enough for comfort, considering Optimal ranges from 18-25, leaving much room for improvement.

Roll call for *Grease*, released 17 February 2017:
>Danny Zuko: Xander York
>Sandy Olsson: Renee Henrich
>Kenickie: Vince Becker
>Frenchie: Gina Forseth
>Vince Fontaine: Johnny Larson
>Betty Rizzo: Helen Trudeau

At her name: Where Helen stops reading.

Excess weight she was in process of losing, was going to lose, was sure to lose goddamnit, by *Grease* opening night 31 March 2017: Only plausible reason for Helen losing starring role to Renee Henrich, Renee again, that pampered little bitch gets everything, even another lead beside Xander, a decision Mrs. Bing will ultimately regret, because one way or another Helen will reveal who she is now, it doesn't have to be in pink jackets or tight black leather, she'll show Mrs. Bing.

Come on, Hel, this is great! Sidekicks are way more fun to play anyway: Gina's encouraging but ultimately uninspiring words to Helen.

Gina's Dominant Behaviors and Traits: Trilling like a bird with delight over small life moments; wearing 1990s boy band concert shirts purchased on eBay; chewing spearmint gum; stating harsh but true words in a brash but ultimately enlightening tone; jumping rope; receiving passable grades in every subject with minimal effort; playing the heel; watching pornography to poke fun at storylines; smiling.

Quit, instead of wasting another minute being underappreciated: What Helen would rather do.

I don't like this new you: Gina's more forceful words upon Helen's declaration.

You know what? Fuck off. You're just jealous: Helen's spiteful words straight to Gina, the friend who has always been by her side, who slept over endless nights and taught Helen samba and hilariously tested the limits of Helen's best toys, Barbie dolls and science kits and numerous Easy-Bake Ovens, before Helen tramps off in opposite direction.

Who has time for silly plays when you're crushing out mileage!: Helen's Facebook post 17 February 2017, recipient of the fewest likes of all her exercise-related posts, causing Helen to cease posting altogether.

Third-pound Golden Cheesy Burger with fries; pounds of fettuccine draped in buttery Alfredo sauce; fried cheese curds dipped in ranch dressing; potato chips of any variety; bucket of fried chicken, breasts and wings and thighs and drummies, the whole damn chicken; movie theater popcorn; cola, any brand, a gigantic, massive cola; whopping dollops of whipped cream atop New York vanilla ice cream, scoops upon scoops, too

many to count, chocolate sauce and strawberry jam drizzling down the sides like a sweet fountain, all atop entire sheet worth of thick fudge-swirled brownies cut into squares salaciously, seductively moist: All Helen can think about that night in bed.

Lake Noquebay: 2,398 acre freshwater Wisconsin lake located between Crivitz and smaller townships of Middle Inlet, Wausaukee, and Loomis. Lake of surprisingly shallow depth excepting a few areas (51' maximum). Fish include panfish, largemouth bass, smallmouth bass, northern pike, trout, and walleye. One of many Wisconsin lakes containing yearly "itch" phenomenon loosely related to bacteria in goose feces. Residence of significant boating and sporting activity in summer (fishing, skiing and tubing, jet-skiing, pontooning, alcohol consuming) and winter (ice fishing, alcohol consuming).

About 25 miles: Perimeter of Lake Noquebay taken on meandering paved and unpaved roads, distance achievable on Helen's Northwoods Springdale 21-speed hybrid bicycle, though not without significant pain in the ass (see *Exercise Side Effects*, *Negative*).

Immense fatigue coupled with a jittery fever: Helen's state post-bike ride, indeed her state after most workouts, the only solution for which is eating something, but Helen knows that's not really a solution at all, that's what fat people do, they solve their problems with food.

Slight pain in stomach: Reaction of Helen's body when she eats right away anyway, which is just trading one problem for another.

Most Important Meal of the Day!: Socially accepted misnomer (see *Common Weight Loss Misconceptions*) applied to breakfast, but also occasionally misapplied to lunch or dinner, the most healthy meal plan involving small caloric intake six or more times daily, making the Most Important Meal of the Day! actually a succession of reduced, responsible meals akin to practiced snacking, the irony lost on most, in that snacking itself is often pegged as the culprit of, not the solution to, weight issues.

Skipping breakfast and lunch: Not preferable but possible, given enough devotion to mantra (see *DO YOU REALLY WANT THIS?*).

Numbers numbers numbers: What comprises much of Helen's life, weight and calories taken in and calories burned and mileage and percentages and meters, now that she has decided to be healthy.

Helen's Dominant Behaviors and Traits, pre-1 November 2016: Acting in school plays; clicking tongue; Netflix binge-watching; playing devil's advocate; thumbs-upping friends' posts on Facebook; reciting lines from previous roles at hilariously snarky times; finding adventure in everyday situations; attempting to impress Xander York; listening; tossing salt over shoulder for luck; baking sugar cookies from scratch; enjoying her parents' company; snacking when hungry.

Helen's Dominant Behaviors and Traits, post-1 November 2016: drinking ≥ eight glasses of water a day; never eating ≤ three hours before bed; seething with self-doubt; running, biking (around Noquebay if clement weather, on Body Blast recumbent if not), Stairmastering, rowing, or other activity that burns quantifiable calories; attempting to gain Xander York's attention with new body; eating less and less each day as a way forward; desiring to quit; dreaming of food.

Daily Schedule, 26 February 2017: (see similar entries for 27 and 28 February, most days March, even weekends extracting class portion of nos 3 and 5):
1. Wake up
2. Skip breakfast
3. Dream about Xander, food during morning classes
4. Skip lunch
5. Dream about food during afternoon classes
6. Body Blast for workout
7. Dream about food while stomaching portions of Elise's dinner in bedroom, alone
8. Immediately catalogue from Julia's Calorie Bible, down to the crumb, day's food intake, drawing a hard double-line underneath to keep from eating more
9. Writhe through restless, dream-filled fits of sleep where fantasies of food and Xander York disturbingly coalesce, where Xander compliments Helen's body while forcing endless supplies of increasingly grotesque food combinations down her throat, barbecued meats deep-fried in donut batter, ice cream topped with grease-slathered bacon, chocolates coated in dripping ketchup-mayo combination.

Lucky Brand Bootleg Princess Jeans, size 6³: What Helen considers trying on again in front of The Mirror, but then that's not really the point anymore, getting back to what she used to be, the point is being better, improving, becoming the thin, beautiful, healthy woman she's never before been.

112.1 lbs.: Weight of Helen Trudeau on 2 March 2017. Final measurement on at-home scale, the next test being the sliding-metal physician scale in high school exercise facility, out in front of everyone, for all to see.

Helen's eating excuses to Elise, to get her the hell off Helen's back, various dates February and March 2017:
1. I've been snacking a lot at school,
2. I just ate a huge lunch,
3. I think I caught that stomach bug again, and
4. I took down a sub sandwich just before you got home.

Helen's Acting Resume: ~~Betty Rizzo (*Grease*)~~; Drizella (*Cinderella*); Madame Thénardier (*Les Misérables*); Chorus Girl (*Little Shop of Horrors*); Ensemble (*Wicked*); Townswoman #4 (*Beauty and the Beast*); Caterpillar (*Hungry Little Caterpillar*); Pig #2 (*Three Little Pigs*).

Opening Night, front and center: Helen's chosen seat for *Grease* on 31 March 2017, in support of Gina but also, as a bonus, a way to showcase new body each time she rises and struts out of theater (seven before intermission, four after), feeling all eyes on her, even Mrs. Bing's; and tell her, Mrs. Bing, who would look better clad in leather and a punk hairdo, serenading and chastising Xander York that he'd better shape up, because she needs a man, and her heart (see various entries for *Helen's Heart*), of course, is set on him.

Renee's ass[2]: Pretty good in the leather, sure, as she turns from her ovation, a standing one, the crowd's jubilance exaggerated, over-the-top, she wasn't that good, Xander mostly carried the duets.

Kyle, Theo, two Vinces: males, both under- and upperclassmen, who compliment Helen after the play.

A bit forced, each tinged with comparison to the past, their subtext saying not *you look great* but *you look different*, comparing Helen to that hideous former version who still exists if they look close enough, still pads her thighs where they refuse to separate, still folds over her bra straps: The compliments.

Helen's Perpetual Love Object: Xander York, the heart-throb, the incomparable, who has yet to compliment Helen.

Common Weight Loss Misconceptions: Eight glasses of water a day; "straight to my hips and/or thighs"; -200 calorie intake $+ -200$ calories burned in exercise $= -$ one pound per week; BMI as indicator of general health; skipping meals; specific areas of body targeted for weight loss; carbohydrates and/or fats and/or proteins excised entirely from diet; calories eaten $\leq$ three hours before bed stored as excess fat; 80/20 rule; weight loss pills; Most Important Meal of the Day!; the Food Pyramid; vibrating abdominal belts; diets.

I think you need help: Words earnestly and softly spoken from Elise to Helen, morning of 3 April 2017.

Are you kidding? I've never felt better. You're just pissed because your time has passed: Helen's defensive response.

Just come home right away from school, okay? I made an appointment with Dr. Samson. Just to talk: Elise's second attempt, even softer and more earnest, if at all possible.

Fuck that! You're just a jealous bitch!: Words too harsh even for Helen but there they are, she's said them, and now she's out the door, on her way to school and finally, finally, to high school exercise facility afterward.

During varsity baseball team's workout: When Helen will go.

Hel, I wanted to——: Words spoken by Gina to Helen as they cross in the hallway after final period, words that Helen ignores entirely, just before entering locker room.

ASICS Gel Kayana shoes, blue and green, size 5.5; FILA Sport Vibrant Workout Pants, black, size XS; Nike Dri-Fit Mesh Racerbank Tank Top, electric pink, size XS; no socks, no underwear, no bra: Helen's never-worn and punctiliously chosen workout attire, modeled countlessly in front of The Mirror, tight-fitting and accentuating in the right places provided she keep peerless posture, breathe sparingly, and refrain from vigorous exercise of any sort, not today, today is only for show, a mild walk and then straight to the scale.

High school exercise facility: Dingier than she'd expected, dark and smelling of piss and old leather, much less appealing than Body Blast but then the atmosphere matters far less than present company.

The stares: What Helen receives from the baseball team, even Coach Gannon, though they fail to meet Helen's expectations, less flattering and more something on which she cannot put her finger.

Xander's compliment: Words that, after wading through the team and other lone underclassmen, Helen finally awaits to adorn her, to hug her body like the form-fitting workout clothes, to simultaneously validate her every mile run, her every calorie counted and discarded, her very being these past months, and also provide motivation to continue on, to never go back to that hideous thing she was (see multiple entries for *Overweight*).

Are you okay?: Words spoken from Xander to Helen.

Thanks Xander, I...: Helen's non sequitur response, Xander's voice crashing against clanging plates and rhythmic treadmill stomps, and even his face, his beautiful face blending with the swaying crowd, arms and legs stretching out like stalks on some vast, never-ending field of flesh and fat and bone and

Remainder of day 3 April 2017, morning and afternoon of 4 April 2017: *This entry has not been verified.*

Blip blip. Blip blip. Blip blip: Distant noise, replacing exercise facility's harmonious blur, of Helen's heartbeat monitor as she wakes in hospital bed, 4 April 2017.

Helen's Heart[3]: Thundering in her chest, every palpitation palpable, every pump strenuous.

Multiple tubes punctured into arms; oxygen mask across face; straps securing arms and torso: Various medical devices imprisoning Helen to bed, impeding speech, movement, or much else than blinking.

88.8 lbs.: Weight of Helen Trudeau on 4 April 2017, recited by Doctor Samson in forbearing voice to Elise and Trent, the eights echoing around the bleached room with ghastly yet not entirely unpleasant symmetry.

Intravenous Feeding: (see also *Parenteral Nutrition*) Reason for the tubes, the only way that Dr. Samson believes Helen can absorb sustenance and begin to gain back what she's lost.

Severe anorexia nervosa, symptoms: Fatigue; hair loss; dry skin; constipation; elevated liver enzymes; brittle nails; low blood pressure; consecutive absences of menstrual cycle (female only); loss of sexual drive (both sexes) leading to impotency (male only); abnormal blood counts; dehydration; seizures; death.

Severe? I think we'd know if our own daughter was that bad: Words offered by Trent, a heartfelt and unsurprising defense, though more of himself than Helen.

Death[2]?: Only word spoken by Elise to Doctor Samson, her voice also resonating through the room, ghastly but with no hint of pleasantness.

112.1 and Renee's ass and Body Blast treadmills and water and 28.5 and Mrs. Bing's disappointed face and Third-pound Golden Cheesy Burger with fries and

sliding scales and Gina's stink-eye and 147.7 and water and Elise's concerned face and leather pants and feeding tubes and 25 miles and water and Xander's smile and the extra extra extra folds of her body: Images and words flashing in Helen's fever dreams as she drifts from Dr. Samson and her parents, as she closes her eyes to the world.

The Arborist's Son

The slow, upheaving pull of Sam's insides feels a bit like uprooting trees with his father's old Ford back in Minnesota. Some of the trees had died of disease—Dutch Elm had swept through like an avaricious tornado in those days—but most had simply traveled where they weren't supposed to go. Roots cracking blacktop, branches poking like children's arms through windows. Unwanted shade. Sam and his twin brother Jake would help load the gear, the chainsaws, the harnesses and straps, and finally the hundred-pound steel chain, fat and slippery like a boa constrictor, into the back of the Ford. Its shocks groaned with the weight. Together the three traveled anywhere within driving distance of town, sometimes three hours or more, to exorcise the offending topiary. Sam didn't then understand the dangers. How, unlike his father, one could take OSHA safety lessons or even Tech school courses. With a hand on their younger brother Garrett's shoulder, their mother offered silent objections that their father countered with a bevy of persuasive, passionate sales pitches, turning on his natural charm. To every job he brought his fifteen-plus years of experience and had endured nothing worse than branch scratches. Jake and Sam could get no better pay elsewhere. On the job, when he would strap up and climb towering trees, rev up a chainsaw and then systematically, trunk piece by trunk piece, chop down what had been growing, spreading, or even dying for decades, both Sam and Jake watched not with trepidation but only with a sense of awed wonder.

The job that day would have been nothing memorable: a line of decorative pines grown disproportionate and ugly. Sam remembers one of them, its base littered with pinkish premature cones, its top branches longer and thicker than the dying ones beneath. It looked like a massive, sad child in an unkempt ghost costume. Sam wanted to pull that one first, but his father insisted, out of some strange need for symmetry, on going outside-in. So while Jake and Sam tied the serpentine chain around the leftmost, sturdiest of the trees, their father backed and anchored the truck into position. Jake hitched the chain, joined Sam at an appropriate distance from it all, and then instantly, for some reason, a reason Sam would search for in the nearly two decades thereafter, the robust chain snapped and whiplashed through the air and, leaping much farther than it seemed it could go, struck Jake right in the chest. He must have flown some distance, but that Sam can't recall. He does remember the sound though, thick and hollow, like a deep, pained breath.

Some seventeen years later, Sam stumbles upon his father's name in the business section of an Arizona phone book. He had been searching for restaurants. The only reason for his trip—indeed, the only reason for most of his travels, his phone conversations, his human contact

in general—is his stage-three lymphoma. Since moving
out at eighteen he has lived nomadically, in all corners
of the country, from North Carolina to Oregon, stints in
Chicago and Boulder and a small town called Oak Ridge
in Montana. But this is his first time in Arizona, and he
has immediate distaste for its dry air and overspiced foods.
He schedules an exit flight for the very afternoon of his
doctor's visit. But then there it is, before he can flip the
page, under *Removals, Arbor and Landscape*: his name,
William Strout and Associates, and the title he'd never held
back in those days: certified arborist.

His logo dominates the quarter-page black-and-white
ad, though it is little more than his name with the Ls as
trees falling apart. In the left-hand corner, his picture sits
unobtrusively. Sam would have missed it if he wasn't
looking. Over the years his cheeks have thinned out, giving
his nose and chin a sharper look. He smiles. Sam searches
for something resembling regret, something resonant of
a life never lived, but the face is indecipherable, the eyes
too small to read.

Though Jake and Sam had been identical, few had trouble
distinguishing them. Jake was stouter, carefree, always on the
move. Sam was the contemplative one, effeminate, more prone
to fits. He let his hair grow while Jake kept his trim. They
exhibited no shared mental acuity either, no surreptitious
communication, no finishing of each other's sentences. If
anything, having another person so molecularly similar to
Sam made Jake's constant presence seem ethereal, left-of-
center. Seeing Jake was like peering into a fun house mirror
that amplified the things Sam didn't want to see.

But then he was gone, and his absence grew even
larger than his presence. Within months their father

abandoned the family and never returned; their mother built a formidable, insulating cocoon of matronly protection around Garrett. Which left Sam, for the years before he escaped cross-state to college, all by himself.

Sam enters the downtown Scottsdale restaurant, a charmingly miniscule place specializing in Sonoran cuisine, around lunchtime. He's not hungry, but he has trained his tongue to tune out flavor the way one might tune out inharmonious music: with an ear for other things. Like with most convictions in life it sometimes worked and sometimes didn't, depending on variables both innumerable and fickle. He orders beans and rice and sopapillas he eats in practiced, child-like bites. Though she has other, more urgent tables, his Latina waitress dotes on him, refreshes his water like clockwork. He thanks her each time.

From his jeans pocket he pulls the torn phone book page. His father's face, his placid smile, is folded at a crease. The doctor's visit did not go well, though at this point, Sam expects little else. There was a time in his life when doctor's visits could offer hues of hope. Now all he receives is varying shades of despair.

He finishes half his plate. The waitress brings him extra napkins he doesn't need. And before he can stop himself, he punches his father's business number in his cellphone and hits send.

Three rings. A woman answers, asks if she can be of assistance. So his company is large enough to employ a secretary. Under the pretext of a potential job, Sam gleans more information from her: four associates alongside his father, seasonal hires during the cooler months, twelfth anniversary of the business this May.

Much of their work is commercial now, profitable a market as that is, but they still take on residential when at all possible.

The fried flatbread knocks at the top of Sam's stomach, threatening to pay a visit up his throat. He sucks at the sweet taste of near-vomit. He has a rather large job, he says between strained breaths. As such, he was wondering if he could speak to William himself.

A pause. She likely looks around her. He may be busy, she says, but she will check. She asks his name and he gives his middle: I am William as well.

She places Sam on hold, her voice replaced by a light rock song eerily reminiscent of Sam's teenage years. The song nears its chorus, an ode to some pop culture goddess, when it abruptly cuts out.

"This is William."

His voice rents Sam's body like a proximate thunderclap. He assumes that Sam hasn't heard him and so repeats, the tremors waving down Sam like a shuddering echo.

"Yes, hello. Sorry." Sam sits up erect in his seat. The waitress circles over, but from his face intuits the importance of his call. She passes. "I'm calling about a job. For a business I own."

"Sounds right up our alley," his father says, the natural salesmanship still in his voice. Behind him a chainsaw howls to life. "What's your business?"

Sam clears his throat as he stumbles into a name, a vocation. Fabrics Galore, a textile business. As he invents, Sam finds himself describing an arboreal amalgam of the places he has worked: a square, brick building surrounded by natural foliage, a small pond. Shaded tree areas where his workers often lunch, guided paths for their breaks. His father asks about square acreage, indigenous and imported flora, potential wildlife, as together they grow Sam's fabricated business. If he recognizes Sam's voice, he gives no indication.

"I can't believe I forgot to ask this," his father says. "Where are you located?"

A straightforward question to which Sam has no answer. The street names of his hotel, the hospital, the restaurant he now occupies all come to mind. But his father, citizen and roving worker of the area for at least a dozen years, will know all these streets and more. He will snuff out a forged map. In the background metal clangs across a floor, and his father is thankfully distracted for a moment.

"You've come highly recommended," Sam says.

"Glad to hear that. We put a lot of pride in our work."

"But I must admit, I'm a bit concerned. Do you work on the weekends?"

"Not unless we have to. Why don't you tell me what you're worried about."

"Well," Sam says. He takes a long, challenging drink of his water. "My employees are everywhere. I'm just wondering, you know, if a few trees are really worth the risk."

Sam takes a needed breath. The chainsaw has stopped, giving way to the mumbled chatter of his employees.

"I'm sorry," his father says. "Let me step into my office."

The line cuts again, to a commercial advertising payday loans. The actor's voice is jumpy, abrasive, so unlike his father's. As the commercial gives way to local weather, then more music, Sam begins to doubt that his father will come back.

But he does return, his voice in a lower octave, the salesmanship gone. Behind him is only silence. "I'm sorry. You were saying?"

"The risks. I'm thinking of the risks."

"There will always be risks," he says. "But we are very good at minimizing them."

"That's good."

"I can promise you, nobody around takes better care than I do. We're safer than driving on the highway."

"Yes. I'm sure you are."

His father sighs. "I can come out for an estimate, if you'd like."

Sam pauses. He closes his eyes. "Yes. I think I would like that."

"Saturday."

Sam contemplates extending his hotel reservation, altering his flight itinerary. He imagines eating days' worth of spicy foods. He realizes how little any of that matters. "Yes, Saturday."

"Great."

Sam hears shuffling on the line, what he mistakes to be his father scrounging for a notepad and pen. He imagines a corded rotary phone, the pig's tail curls stretched taut. But then abruptly, without warning, the line clicks and goes dead. Sam loses his grip on his phone. It clatters against the table. His father hadn't asked again for the address, or a phone number. He hadn't asked for a way to get back to Sam.

Building Faith

"Y ou think it's one of those altar boy jobs?" Gary asks. Wyatt Brennan leans his chest into a ladder rung and wipes sweat from his brow with a gloved hand. He looks at his younger brother Gary nestled in his harness, holding a nail gun in one hand and his share of a two-by-four in the other. Behind him, in a hole where a wall should be, plastic garbage bags duct taped together flap like flames in a southeastern wind.

"Nope," Wyatt says. "Not indulging you. Not today."

Gary nods toward the back of the church, where Father Mason, thin and prematurely bald and baby-faced, walks with a black-haired boy no more than ten years old. The two stop as Father Mason proselytizes at one of the Passions hanging on the good, upheld east wall. He gesticulates with aplomb. The paintings are massive, marble-framed and medieval-looking, even though the artist is still alive and is currently somewhere in Mexico at work on the west wall replacements. Father Mason then places a hand on the boy's nearest shoulder and continues their walk, toward the confessional box and out of sight.

Wyatt looks back at his brother, larger in size and in many ways looking the older. Gary flashes one of his devilish smirks. "Only saying."

"No, Gare, you're insinuating. Now hammer in that board. Sick of waiting on you."

"Hey, look," Gary says, pointing his nail gun at Wyatt in accusation. "I know why you're testy today. But don't take it out on me."

Gary leans back carelessly and squints one eye, reeling the corded nail gun back as though it is nothing more than his fist. Without measuring or leveling he hammers forward three perfectly placed nails.

"You want to know what I think?" Gary asks.

The air compressor revs into the echoing church. Wyatt extends his arm to accept the gun from his brother. He eyeballs his crossing and delivers three more nails, not as precise as Gary but sturdy enough. The board seems a shade long, and so Wyatt pulls a piece of sandpaper and shaves it down as best he can. Hooking the gun to a higher ladder rung, he climbs down toward the lumber pile.

"I already know what you think," Wyatt says. "It's one hell of a coincidence is what it is. Not a damn thing more."

"Bite that tongue, Wy. You're in the House of God." Gary leans back into his harness and raises a hand behind his head, as though he is relaxing on some beach. "But you're wrong. This is no coincidence. This is some kind of reverse miracle or something."

"It's business, all that matters." Wyatt hunches over the pile of boards. "How long you cut these?"

"Eighteen, five seven-sixteenths. What you think?"

Wyatt extends his tape measure and glides it down the top of a board. Eighteen feet, five inches and a half. "Off a sixteenth."

"Who cares? Not like they need to last anyhow, huh?"

Wyatt retracts his tape, contemplating bringing all the boards back outside just to shave off something that won't make much of a difference. He doesn't agree with his brother about the church's fortunes but he has to admit that history might. This most recent repair is the third massive job in as many years that Sacred Heart Parish has contracted for the brothers. The first year had been a tornado, the first officially recorded in the normally placid town of Kimberly. That small funnel struck the north wing of the church, scattering the entire priest's quarters, altar, and half the pews in all directions. Just two weeks after the Brennans finished the extensive repairs an accidental candelabra fire set the front doors and the foyer area ablaze, the diabolical flames fighting a valiant three-hour battle against local firemen. After the Brennans provided all new Grecian-style doorways, including sturdy stone pillars guaranteed never to go up in flames, and a tiled entryway, Sacred Heart enjoyed eight months of peace. The worst seemed behind them. Father Mason delivered a poignant Sunday sermon likening the church's endurance against adversity to the Passion itself. The next day a cold front from the west met unseasonably humid air from the south, causing the second tornado in Kimberly history to touch down half a mile from the church. The obstinate twister skimmed county roads, zig-zagged through cornfields, just far enough to explode the abandoned barn across the street and send its weathered boards straight through Sacred Heart's west wall.

In the *Post-Crescent* the following morning, reporters speculated that the church might be doomed. When interviewed Father Mason simply said, "Christ fell three times, and three times he rose." After a week the Brothers

Brennan Contractors received the call and made their
yearly pilgrimage out to Sacred Heart to do the good work.

"These things don't just happen," Gary says.
"Especially not to churches."

Wyatt lifts three boards and stands them on end. Gary
grabs hold as Wyatt again makes toward the ladder.

Father Mason's voice echoes about the church and
reaches the brothers in murmurs. As Wyatt ascends the
ladder with the boards in one hand, Gary picks at a piece
of tape securing the church's plastic, temporary shelter
from unforeseen natural forces.

"Reminds you of those beat-up Chevys the Andersons
used to drive, doesn't it?" Gary asks as much to himself.
"Shatter the glass for sport it seemed like. Then they'd
drive all squint-eyed until one of them wrapped an
oak tree."

"It reminds me of this place."

"That's because you have no imagination, brother."

Just then Father Mason reenters the main hall with a
man in a business suit. He has impeccable shoes and long,
ponytailed blond hair. Father Mason laughs with
enthusiasm at the man's words. They walk together, with
a familiar stride. Wyatt watches them briefly but turns
back to his task, lifting the gun and adjusting the board
only to find that Gary hasn't held up his end.

"The upside," Wyatt says. "At this pace we'll still be
here when the next disaster hits."

"Maybe it's insider trading," Gary says, his eyes still
fixed on the blond man. "Maybe Father dipped his hand
into the offering plate one too many times and God's
pissed."

"Keep your voice down."

"Mafia ties? Seems a little HBO, but you never know."

"Christ, Gare. The man's probably his brother."

"Brother? Father's bald as a baby and that guy's freaking Fabio."

Gary eyeballs the board to level and nods the go-ahead to Wyatt. Wyatt hits three nails in but the board still bulges, shimmies a bit with a tug, and so he stabilizes it with two more.

"Wasting nails, Wy," Gary says. "And you're calling me distracted. Are we gonna at least acknowledge that the wedding is happening?"

"No."

Father Mason and the man take up the farthest pew, their mouths moving soundlessly under the drum of the air compressor. Occasionally the two men look over to the brothers but only as a fleeting stop on the path of their generally trouping eyes. Wyatt has to admit that, during their three-year engagement, the Brennans and Father Mason have kept a distant business relationship. As a priest he is conspicuous, somewhat omniscient himself, always present but rarely near them, speaking to Wyatt and Gary once a day if at all. Sure, they aren't parishioners like much of the community, but haven't they come through for the church in times of crises? Aren't they the reason that the church rises after each fall? In some ways the Brennans build the church the way parishioners build faith, with blind optimism for the future because really, what's the alternative? Hell, the work they did the first year was nothing short of a miracle. It would have taken larger contractors twice the time and triple the manpower to finish what Wyatt and Gary did in eight months of fourteen-hour workdays. And so, unlike many of Gary's conspiratorial fancies, these church-related ones may not be unfounded. What building crumbles under three separate natural disasters in as many years while the town surrounding it remains relatively unscathed?

But Wyatt can't encourage these thoughts, especially today. In a different Catholic church hundreds of miles away in Minnesota, his ex-wife Cheryl will remarry. Their seven-year-old son Cody, ring bearer at his mother's own wedding, dressed in a little tuxedo, will break the congregation's heart. Those years ago when he and Cheryl mutually decided on divorce, he had conceded primary custody of Cody without much fight. Cheryl was a good mother, but more than that, he wanted to spare his son the unyielding travel, the meandering diaspora that he and Gary had to go through. He wanted Cody to have a singular home. And if Wyatt is willing to follow Gary's perverse ruminations on divine retribution now, he must also account for the myriad missteps that he took away from his own son's life. He must assume not that Cheryl and he were simply incompatible, but that he had done something irreparably wrong. That he deserves this lonesome fate.

So maybe there's no reason behind the disasters that have rent Sacred Heart or his life. Maybe the inexplicable is just that.

"Oh yeah," Gary says, "Chewy called. Shipment won't be in until Thursday now. Said two drivers up and walked out last week. One of them unzipped and pissed all over his empty locker. Believe that?"

"Thursday. He knows that order was meant for a week ago, right?"

"Yeah. So what? Give my ass a chance to spend some quality time with my couch. They pay us by job not hour. Remember whose great business idea that was?"

Wyatt ignores his brother. The blond man has gone; Father Mason emerges from the back of the church alone. He saunters with his hands behind his back and his head ululating, as though he is in some imaginary meadow. Gary shakes his head, lines up the second of the boards and says something while driving the nails home.

"Can't hear you when you're hitting," Wyatt says.

Gary leans in, his bulk testing the strength of the rope harness. Wyatt has warned him of shifting too often but his brother won't have it, and he certainly won't agree to be the runner.

"I said, there's something about that guy."

"Okay. Or maybe, like everything else, you get some idiotic idea in your head and suddenly it's truth."

"Look, I know, it sucks." Gary looks to Wyatt, his eyes showing his otherwise hidden youth. "But remember that you chose this. You could've fought harder for Cody but you didn't."

"Fuck off, Gare. You don't know anything about it."

"Then, please, like I said before: don't take it out on me."

Just then three teenage girls enter the church and stand sheepishly at the penultimate pew. At first Father Mason doesn't notice them. The brothers watch the group as they fidget with glossy nails and in meager purses. The tallest of them, a girl with hair the color of fire, brushes some defiant substance off another's shoulder. Each is dressed for the heat, T-shirts or loose tank tops, frayed hand-cut jean shorts or skirts.

When Father Mason notices the girls he hastens his steps and greets each one with an outreached hand. After an exchange he ushers the girls down the aisle, the click of their footsteps coalescing into a rhythmic hymn even the air compressor can't drown out.

Wyatt watches the girls traipse the aisle, Father Mason in front of them, his head forward and his lips in a half-smile. He chooses a pew and they follow, sitting down beside him as though they are kin awaiting the start of mass. Gary shoots Wyatt one of his smiles.

"Don't go there," Wyatt says. "Do not even think about it."

Halcyon

Her mission is simple: to swim straight across Noquebay, a lake neither wide at its center nor deep, save a fifty-foot drop-off that ends almost as soon as it begins. Of course, when she proclaims this to her family at dinner, her quest produces laugher from her older brother Ian, skeptic worry from her mother, and stern denial from her father. Plenty of ways for a teenager to die, he muses, and trying to do something so stupid as swim across a lake for no goddamn reason certainly doesn't need to be one of them. After short silence Hunter attempts her rebuttal. First, the opposing shoreline isn't even far, with the trees, the cottages, the two beaches all in clear view. Second, the lake isn't even deep, and excepting a few parts, Hunter can practically walk across the thing. Third, and most important, she has been swimming since before she could walk. And finally a question: how, she wants to know, is this any different than surfing in high waves or hiking up a mountain? Brave people do this kind of thing every day.

Her mother sets down her fork. Her father takes his napkin from his lap. He waits for Hunter's excitement to abate. When it doesn't—when Hunter begins rephrasing points already made—he abruptly cuts in.

"Are you done?" he asks. Before Hunter can reply he says, "Good, because this is the last I hear of this."

The next day, while her father sits in front of his evening hour of news, her mother at the jigsaw puzzle on the folding table, and her brother long gone with friends, Hunter stands at the patio door leading from her house to Noquebay. At night the lake is vast and dark. She can almost feel its quiescent power. Then she does feel something: her mother's hand, gently atop her shoulder.

"Do you remember the time with the lifejackets?"

Her mother then recounts the story Hunter has heard a hundred times over, when Hunter and Ian and their cousin Nate fastened lifejackets around their ankles as an aberrant way to make lake tag more challenging. Her mother speaks with listless eyes about Hunter flipping over, kicking and flailing in panic, but how Ian and Nate believed it just a ruse to lure them closer. How Hunter lost consciousness. The CPR, the hospital. The dogged surveillance of any water activities thereafter.

"I know, Mom," Hunter says. "I know."

"But you can't know," she says. "You have no idea what it's like to be a parent. Your father and I—we just want you to be safe."

"Me too."

She kisses the crown of Hunter's head. "I know it looks unassuming, but that lake can still harm you. It's still a massive body of water."

"Yeah, Mom, I got it."

Hunter leaves for her bedroom, leery of more stories of her dubious youth, or even worse, the multitudinous tall tales passed along the lake through generations. She has heard all of these too, from so many different sources, gossip and facts intertwining into local fables. Among the lake's alleged prey were a young girl, a group of drunk college roommates, a father and his only son. Boaters, swimmers, fishermen trapped under the ice. This person's brother knew so-and-so who knew the neighbors of one of the drowned. Hunter knows all the macabre legends of Lake Noquebay's unquenchable thirst and believes none of them. Their myths exist as a cautionary tale meant to frighten and deter dreamers like Hunter. And deterred she simply refuses to be.

A week later, under the guise of darkness, Hunter embarks. The day has been seasonably calm, with wind whispering in short, gasped spurts, as though Mother Nature cannot quite catch her breath. Naked, Hunter lifts her first-story bedroom window and escapes without sound. She slides her sleek wetsuit over her lissome body as she wades into the rocky shore beside her father's dock. The water sends a soft shiver into her legs. She looks down the shoreline that loses itself to darkness on both sides. Then up to the cloudless night sky, the countless stars. As she proceeds the depth of the water shallows before it deepens, a Noquebay distinction Hunter has known her entire life. Then begins the gradual drop, and soon she is submerged to her chest. The moonlight ripples jagged across the surface, a yellow brick road leading to her Oz. Taking a deep breath, one that feels it could take her straight across the lake, she admits herself completely into the water. She proceeds with a single thought: I am Hunter Oberlin, Noquebay, and I will conquer you.

The water is cool, pitch-black. When she opens her eyes underneath she can see no farther than her elbows, and yet she can sense the presence of life around her, minnows and fish darting away from her midnight invasion. She glides in large practiced strokes, taking each as they come. Forward crawl to doggie-paddle, backstroke to breast. This is how water is meant to be experienced, Hunter's every stroke pushing away one thing and revealing another, drawing back with her fingertips curtain after curtain, each leading into new and undiscovered rooms. As the distant shore grows closer, she sees herself standing atop its sand in a jubilant fatigue. Feeling the accomplishment that can only accompany utter exhaustion. The walk back across the shoreline will be long but peaceful. She will hang her wetsuit in its place below the deck and never wear it again. In the morning her parents will be none the wiser, but Ian, sagacious Ian will see it in her eyes. He will need to know. Hunter will withhold her tale at first, suspend him in quizzical wonder, until the time is just right to unveil her masterpiece.

A northern wind incites waves that bring Hunter her first hints of fatigue. Her shoulder smarts, remnant of a soccer injury two years ago. She decides to allow herself a minor break. She sinks and resurfaces in short intervals. But when she dips one last time and kicks to continue it is cumbersome, entangled in a thick, paste-like feel. It gives no pleasure. The next few kicks the same. She tries to calm herself, to take it slowly, but then her lungs request air, as do her anxious arms. She kicks more rapidly and her body raises its demands. Her throat burns. She feels confined by some invisible force; all she needs is to break through it and propel upward, back to where she was, where she came from. Just one determined push. She sees her mother, cooking dinner over the stove, asking about everyone's day in her perpetual concern. And her father, his eyes on the television. Ian waxing intellectual about the superiority of La Liga. She needs to fight through, to take control. Just needs to reach the surface, the moonlight and the stars, to break out, to break free, to break

And then, all at once, it stops.

She does not kick. Her lungs and limbs no longer burn. Her arms lift effortlessly and float about her body. Below, around, above her is pure black. But almost instantly, Hunter notices an aureate glow that she recognizes as a heart, a secret: she has come face-to-face with the moonlike luminescence of the deep lake. Just as she releases herself to it, some unforeseen force tugs her arm, its grasp fiery on her wrist. Her body surges to the tug as she loses consciousness.

At the hospital they run many tests. She is deemed physically stable but must stay an extra day for psychiatric counseling. She hates the prepackaged food and cannot shake a cloudy, floating headache. The discordant echo of water in her ears. Ian and her mother remain all day; her father comes and goes. Each new room the nurses usher her into feels overstuffed and stifling. She has trouble breathing.

Back at home her father installs a security system and disallows Hunter and Ian the passcode. Against her shrillest objections he nails her window shut. Her parents sleep lightly, never far from wakeful consciousness, appearing from their room if Hunter so much as uses the bathroom. Through bleary eyes they talk of moving.

Hunter resents the imprisonment, this treatment like an insubordinate, disaster-prone child. Ian, the one who saved her, remains omnipresent. She treats his ubiquity like a flu-ridden person will a blanket: at times thankfully enwrapped and at others harshly, scornfully dismissive. During those feverish fits she stands at the patio door and peers out at the crystalline lake, in awe of what it almost took from her, its timid power. In those moments she succumbs to the siren song of senescent waves crashing against the shoreline, their symphony right there in her backyard, calling out to her, waiting.